The
2nd
Big Big
Book of

Allen & Unwin
83 Alexander St
Crows Nest NSW 2065
Australia
Phone:    (61 2) 8425 0100
Fax:      (61 2) 9906 2218
Email:    info@allenandunwin.com
Web:      www.allenandunwin.com

National Library of Australia

Cataloguing-in-Publication details are available from the National
Library of Australia
www.librariesaustralia.nla.gov.au

The text in this book is printed on
Australian made ENVI Carbon Neutral paper.
ENVI Carbon Neutral paper is certified by the Australian Government.
Cover and series design by Sandra Nobes
Typeset in Sabon by Toucan Design
Collection repagination by Midland Typesetters, Australia
This book was printed in March 2010 at McPherson's Printing Group
76 Nelson Street, Maryborough, Victoria 3465, Australia
www.mcphersonsprinting.com.au

10 9 8 7 6 5

The
2nd
Big Big
Book of

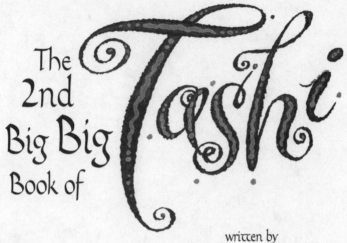

written by
**Anna Fienberg**
and **Barbara Fienberg**

illustrated by
**Kim Gamble**

**ALLEN&UNWIN**

*It's about time to confess that Tashi is as familiar, beloved (and sometimes annoying) as any family member. It's true. How many times a day do we talk about him, wonder what on earth will happen to him next? 'What would Tashi do?' we ask each other desperately in a crisis. You could try this too, if you like, because it's actually quite a handy way to solve problems. Even though Tashi is small and not very old, he comes up with some cunning plans in tight situations. Which just goes to show that if you use your brains you can overcome Wicked Barons and beastly Bluebeards, haunted houses and heartless kidnappers, plus you'll learn how to hold on when you really, really need to pee...*

*So, here you go, a big, big dose of Tashi! If you read this enormous book through, young Tashi just might become a member of your family too – he'd like that.*

ANNA AND BARBARA FIENBERG

Anna and Barbara Fienberg write the Tashi stories together. Kim Gamble is one of Australia's favourite illustrators for children. Together Kim and Anna have made such wonderful books as *The Magnificent Nose and Other Marvels*, *The Hottest Boy Who Ever Lived*, the *Tashi* series, the *Minton* picture books, *Joseph*, and a full colour picture book about their favourite adventurer, *There once was a boy called Tashi*.

# Contents

# Tashi

## and the
## DANCING
## SHOES

written by
**Anna Fienberg**
and
**Barbara Fienberg**
•

illustrated by
**Kim Gamble**

**ALLEN&UNWIN**

One Saturday, Jack invited Tashi for lunch to meet his Uncle Joe.

'He's my father's brother,' Jack told him proudly. 'He's been travelling all over the world.'

'That's interesting,' said Tashi. 'I wonder if he's ever been to *my* village.'

'We'll ask him,' Jack said excitedly. 'You can swap stories about snake-infested forests and wild escapes from war lords. It'll be great!'

Tashi and Joe did have a lot to talk
about. They talked all through the soup,
well into the beef with noodles, pausing
only when the apple cake was served.

'It's very good to meet an uncle of yours,
Jack,' said Tashi, taking a bite of his cake.
'Have you got any more?'

'There's some in the kitchen,' said Mum,
hopping up.

'He meant *uncles*, Mum,' laughed Jack.
'You know, if we asked all *yours* to lunch,
Tashi, we'd have to hire the town hall!'

Tashi nodded. 'It's true. But I'll tell you
something. No matter if you have forty
uncles and fifty-six aunts and nine hundred
and two cousins, all of them are precious.'
He sighed. 'Take Lotus Blossom, for
example.'

'Who's that?' asked Dad, scratching his
head. 'An uncle?'

Tashi scooped up the last of his cake. 'No, Lotus Blossom is my cousin. We used to play chasings near the river in summer. *Wah*, was she a fast runner! Nearly quicker than *me!* She'd go streaking off on her own then hide in the tiniest, most impossible places. I'd take ages to find her.'

Tashi finished up his cake and pushed back his chair. 'So when they told me Lotus Blossom had disappeared, I wasn't too worried. At first, that is.'

Uncle Joe leaned forward. 'Disappeared, eh?' He nodded knowingly. 'What was it? Bandits, war lords, *kid*nappers?'

Dad winked at Jack. 'Here we go!' he whispered, bouncing on his chair.

'Well, it was like this,' began Tashi. 'One afternoon, my mother and I had just come back from a visit to Wise-as-an-Owl, when there was a furious knocking at the door and Lotus Blossom's grandmother, Wang Mah, stumbled in. Her face was wet with tears and strands of hair from her bun were plastered across her cheeks.

'"I've lost her!" Wang Mah burst out. "One minute my dear little Lotus Blossom was playing in the courtyard right next to me – the *next*, she was gone!" She wrung her hands. "Oh, what will happen when night falls?"

'My mother sat her down on a chair.

'"I was just painting my screen," Wang Mah went on. "You know, the one with the Red Whiskered Dragon? Well, I couldn't get the green right on the scales – "

'"Where did you look for her?" I interrupted.

'Wang Mah threw up her hands. "Oh, everywhere! The fields, the cemetery – I've told the whole village, practically. Everyone's out looking, but no one can find her. Oh, my little one, where could she be?"

'Well, I knew we wouldn't find her sitting there in the house worrying, so I told my mother that I was going to join the search party and that I would be back later.

'"Oh, thank you, Tashi," cried Wang
Mah. "If anyone can find her, you will,
I know."

'I wasn't so sure, but I crossed my fingers
and gave her the sign of the dragon for luck.
But as I walked towards the village square,
a cold fear was settling in my stomach.
Whenever Grandmother was painting one of
her screens, she didn't hear or see anything
else for hours. Lotus Blossom might have
been missing since dawn. So I decided to go
at once to the village fortune teller.'

Uncle Joe nodded wisely. 'I went to one last year, when I was back in the tropics. Did I ever tell you about the time – '

'Yes,' said Dad quickly.

'So, Tashi,' said Mum, 'did the fortune teller have any news?'

'Well, it was like this. Luk Ahed had done horoscope charts for everyone in our village, so I thought he might give us a clue about Lotus Blossom. Luk Ahed is very good at telling the future, but not so brilliant at keeping things tidy. He rummaged through great piles of sacred books and maps of the stars and bamboo sticks. But he couldn't find her horoscope anywhere.

'"I'll start on a new one right away,"
he promised. Then he grunted with
surprise. He had *my* chart in his hand.

'"Just look at this," he marvelled. "I see
a great adventure awaiting you, Tashi, just
as soon as you find a very special pair of
red shoes with green glass peacocks
embroidered on them."

'I walked out of there very thoughtfully,
I can tell you. I could almost remember
seeing such a pair of shoes, but where? As
I turned the corner into the village I heard
the familiar rat-a-tat-tat coming from the
shoemaker's shop.

'"Hello, Tashi," Not Yet called from his
open door. Our cobbler was called Not Yet
because no matter how long people left
their shoes with him, when they returned
to see if they were ready, he always said,
"Not yet. Come back later."

12

'Well, I stopped right there on the doorstep. Of course, *that's* where I'd seen those strange shoes. I ran into the shop and asked Not Yet if he still had them.

'"I think so," said Not Yet. "I know the ones you mean. They were here when I took over this shop from my father years ago." He poked around at the back of the shelves and finally fished out a dusty pair of shoes. He wiped them clean with his sleeve.

'The shoes were just as I remembered. They were red satin and glowed in the dingy room. I took some coins from my pocket and asked, "Could I take them now?"

'Not Yet look at the worn soles and heels and clicked his tongue. "Not yet," he said. "Come back later."

'So I went down to the river for a while and looked along the banks and in our usual hiding places for any sign of Lotus Blossom. After an hour, without a speck of dragon luck, I returned to the shop.

'"Be careful with them, Tashi," Not Yet said as he handed the shoes to me. "Be *very* careful." And he looked at me in a worrried way.

'Clutching them tightly to my chest,
I ran as fast as I could to the edge of the
village. The shoes glowed like small twin
sunsets in my hand. When I stopped and
put them on, my feet began to grow hot
and tingle. I gave a little hop. At least
I meant to give a little hop, but instead
it was a great whopping *leap*, followed by
another and another, even higher. I couldn't
help laughing, it felt so strange. I ran a few
steps, but each step was a huge bound. In
a few seconds I had crossed the fields and
was down by the river again.

'Well, even though I was so worried about Lotus Blossom, I have to tell you I couldn't help being excited about the shoes.'

'Who could?' cried Dad. 'No one would blame you for that!'

'So I decided to run home – just for a minute, you know – and show my family. But those shoes had other ideas! They went on running in quite the opposite direction: over the bridge and into the forest. I tried to stop, but the shoes wouldn't let me. I tried to kick them off, but they were stuck fast to my feet. I was getting very tired, and a little bit scared.'

'Who wouldn't be?' said Dad.

'Even I, with my vast experience, would be alarmed by the situation,' put in Uncle Joe.

'Yes, and then I saw the long shadows of the trees and the deepening dusk. Soon it would be dark, and I didn't know where on earth the shoes were taking me.

'Just then I heard a shout. The shoes bounded on and stopped suddenly near the edge of a deep pit. A tiger pit! I shivered deep inside. I'd had quite enough of tigers, remember, when I was trapped with one in that wicked Baron's storeroom.'

'Old Baron *bogey*,' muttered Dad.

'A voice yelped again, "Is anyone there?" And do you know, it was Lotus Blossom!

'"Yes, it's me, Tashi!" I called, and the shoes moved forward. I leaned over the side of the pit. "Hello, Lotus Blossom. How did you come to fall down there? You weren't *hid*ing, were you?"

'"No!" yelled Lotus Blossom, stamping her foot. "It's no joke being down here. I got lost, and I was running, and there were branches over the pit so you couldn't see it. Oh, Tashi, I've been here all day, so frightened that a tiger might come and fall in on top of me."

'I jerked back and shot a look over my shoulder. But what could I do? I had no rope or any means of getting her up. Then my toes tingled inside the shoes, reminding me. Yes! My splendid magic shoes could take me home in no time and I would be back with a good long rope as quick as two winks of an eye.

'But at that moment Lotus Blossom began to scream. My heart thumped as I saw a large black snake slithering down into the hole, gliding towards her.

'I didn't have time to think. The shoes picked me up and jumped me down into the pit. *Wah!*

'Maybe I'll land on the snake and squash him, I thought. But no, the snake heard me coming and slid to one side. I landed with a crash.

'"Hide behind me, Lotus Blossom," I said, facing the serpent. Lotus Blossom did as I told her, but doesn't she always have to have the last word? She picked up rocks and threw them at the snake, shouting *"WAH! PCHAAA!"*

'"Leave him, Lotus Blossom!" I whispered, but it was too late. The snake was enraged. It drove us back into the corner, lunging fiercely.

'"Put your arms around my waist and hold on," I told Lotus Blossom.

'No sooner had she done so than my feet began to tingle. The magic shoes jumped me straight up the steep side of the pit and out into the clean, fresh air.

'I hoisted Lotus Blossom onto my shoulders and with a few exciting bounds we were back in the village square. The bell was rung to call back the searchers, and you should have seen them racing joyfully towards us! They swept Lotus Blossom up into their arms, clapping and cheering like thunder. Wang Mah grabbed her, and scolded and wept, her long white hair tangling them both together. But when the crowd saw me doing one of my playful little leaps – well, *flying* right over their heads! – they gasped in amazement.

'"Look at those shoes! Where did he get them? Look at him fly!" they cried.

'I was just taking my bow when I spied a face in the crowd that I had hoped never to see again: my greedy Uncle Tiki Pu.'

'Oh, *him!*' Jack turned to Uncle Joe. 'He's the worst uncle ever. When he came to stay with Tashi, he threw all the toys out the window to make way for his things!'

'I just brought my pyjamas and a change of underpants for the weekend,' said Uncle Joe quickly. 'Is that all right?'

'When the crowd drifted away,' Tashi went on, 'I walked home. I was feeling very gloomy, muttering to myself, when suddenly Tiki Pu's shadow loomed over me. He was rubbing his hands together with glee, and my heart sank. But I needn't have worried about him coming to *stay* – that was going to be the least of my problems.

'"You must come to the city with me, Tashi," he said, gripping my shoulder hard. "I know the Emperor well. Er, not the Emperor himself, perhaps, but certainly his Master of Revels. He could arrange for you to dance at the Palace. We will make our fortunes!"

'*We* will! *Our* fortunes? I thought.

'Tiki Pu was very insistent, never letting me have any peace with all his jawing on – "imagine, the *Em*peror, the *Em*peror!" – so in the end I agreed to go.

'The next morning, Tiki Pu stood on my toes (yes, it hurt, but at least it was quick) and off we bounded. It was amazing – a journey that took days of normal walking was over in half an hour. Suddenly, there we were at the front door of the Emperor's Master of Revels.

'The Master didn't look too pleased to
see Uncle Tiki Pu. But after he had watched
me do six somersaults from one leap, and
dance up one wall, across the ceiling and
down the other side, he clapped Tiki Pu on
the shoulder.

'"The Emperor is giving a grand dinner
tonight," he said. "The boy will dance for
him at the Palace."

'"Will the Princess Sarashina be there?"
I asked.

'"No, she is away visiting her aunt," the Master of Revels called over his shoulder as he hurried away to make the arrangements. Then he stopped. I saw him look back at me, and a sly expression came over his face. His eyes narrowed into a mean smile.

'We had only gone a little way when the Master came after us. He had two huge evil-looking guards with him.

'"Take those shoes from the boy," the Master ordered. "They should fit my son perfectly. He will be much more graceful. Why should *this* clumsy oaf have the honour of dancing before the Emperor!"

'"The Master's honourable son will bring him glory and gold!" said the first guard.

'"Praise and presents!" said the second guard.

'"The shoes won't come off," I said loudly. "I've *tried*."

'The guards rushed at me and pushed and pulled, but they couldn't remove the shoes.

'"Oh, well – chop off his feet!" ordered the Master. "We can dig his toes out of the shoes later."

'I looked desperately at my uncle. Tiki Pu took a very small step forward. "Ah," he stammered. "You shouldn't really, I mean to say, that's not very – "

'"Be quiet," snapped the Master, "or we will chop off his head, and yours as well."

'Tiki Pu stepped back quickly. "Oh, in that case . . . "

'Some uncle, I thought bitterly.

'The guard drew out his mighty sword and swung it up above his head . . . But before he could bring it down, the door flew open and Princess Sarashina burst into the room.

'"What are you doing?" she cried. "Put that sword down at once. This is Tashi, the boy who rescued me from the demons and saved my life! Just as well I came back early, Tashi. What a way to repay your kindness." She scolded the Master of Revels and his guards out of the room.

'Well, I was never so glad to see anyone
in my whole life. So when the Princess
invited me to take tea with her, I followed
her into a beautiful room all hung about
with silks and tapestries, and we talked
and laughed until nightfall.

'That evening I danced for the Emperor
and the Court. I twirled high over people's
heads and swooped and ducked and glided
like a bird.

'"Miraculous!" they cried, throwing coins at me, which Uncle Tiki Pu hastily gathered up. The Emperor gave me a nice little bag of gold for my trouble, but Tiki Pu was at my side at once. He whisked the bag from my hand.

'"I'll keep this safe for you, Tashi my boy," he beamed, as he slipped it into his pocket.

'"Is there anything else I can do for you, Tashi?" the Emperor asked.

'"Not for me, your Highness, but there is something my uncle would dearly like."

'Tiki Pu pricked up his ears and gave me a toothy grin.

'"And what is that, my boy?" the Emperor smiled.

'"My uncle has always had a great desire to travel." Out of the corner of my eye I saw that Tiki Pu looked very surprised. I whispered something in the Emperor's ear.'

'What? What?' cried Dad.

'I know, I know!' cried Uncle Joe.

'Well, the next day I returned home alone and went straight at once to see Luk Ahed, the fortune teller. "You were right about the shoes," I said, "but I've had enough adventures for the time being, and I'm so tired. Can you tell me how to take them off?"

'"Nothing could be easier," said Luk Ahed. "All you have to do is twirl around three times, clap your hands and say, Off shoes!"

'I followed his instruction and oh, the relief to wiggle my toes in the cool dust. I carried the shoes home and carefully put them in the bottom of my playbox.

'"And Tiki Pu hasn't come back with you?" my mother asked when I told her about the grand dinner and the Emperor and Princess Sarashina.

'"No, he couldn't. A ship was leaving the next morning for Africa and the Emperor thought that it was too good an opportunity for Tiki Pu to miss, seeing he likes travel so much."

'My mother gave me one of her searching looks. "What a clever Tashi," she said at last, and smiled.'

There was a little silence at the table. Then Dad snorted loudly. 'Some uncle, all right, that Tiki Pu. Of all the lily-livered, cowardly . . . You wouldn't say *he* was a precious relative, would you, Tashi?'

'About as precious as a crocodile hanging off your leg!' put in Uncle Joe.

'He may have met a few by now,' grinned Tashi. 'Crocodiles are quite common in Africa, aren't they?'

'So I believe,' said Joe. 'In fact once, when I was in a typical African forest,

I saw a crocodile grab the muzzle of a zebra. Pulled him into the river, easy as blinking. Dreadful sight. A Nile crocodile, it was. Notorious man-killers. Did I tell you about the time . . . ?'

And so Tashi stayed till dusk crept in all over the table and Dad had to put the lights on and Tashi's mother called him home for dinner.

'Come back tomorrow, young fellow!' urged Uncle Joe. 'I'm cooking *crocodile!*'

## THE FORTUNE TELLER

'Funny how crocodile tastes almost exactly like chicken,' remarked Dad.

'Yes, same chewy white meat,' said Mum.

Uncle Joe stared very hard at his plate. 'Actually,' he said, after a long pause, 'they were out of crocodile at the supermarket. Fancy! In Tiabulo, where I've just come from, you can buy it everywhere: canned, baked, boiled . . . Great for late night suppers when the fish aren't jumping.'

35

'Thank the stars we don't live in Tiabulo,'
Dad whispered to Jack, behind his hand.

It was Sunday, and the family were
sitting down to lunch. It was a late lunch
because Uncle Joe had taken ages to cook
it, but Tashi had only just arrived. He'd
been making the dessert.

'Have you ever tried ghost pie?' asked
Tashi. 'It's a secret recipe learned from
ghosts I once knew.'

'No,' said Uncle Joe, 'but I remember
a fortune teller once said – '

'Luk Ahed?' asked Jack.

'No, another one, in the Carribean
Islands. Anyway, this man told me that
when I was forty-three I would visit my
brother and meet a wise young lad who
would offer me a most mysterious dessert.'

'Aha!' Dad smacked his forehead. 'Ghost pie! Eat a slice and walk through walls. What's more mysterious than that? Your fortune came true then, didn't it?'

'Sometimes it does,' Tashi said slowly, 'and sometimes it doesn't.'

Jack looked hard at Tashi. 'Did you go back and see *your* fortune teller?'

Tashi nodded. 'Yes, and it wasn't long before I wished I'd never stepped foot in the place.' He put his fork down. 'Luk Ahed had been so clever telling me about the magic shoes, I decided to visit him again. I thought maybe he'd find some more surprises in my horoscope.'

'And *did* he?' asked Dad eagerly.

'You can *bet* on it,' said Uncle Joe, playing hard with his peas. 'They always do.'

'More than I'd ever bargained for,' agreed Tashi. 'See, it was like this. Luk Ahed was just finishing his breakfast when I arrived, but he put down his pancake and licked his fingers. He was like that – always happy to see you, always eager to help. It was only a few days since my last visit to him, so my chart hadn't been completely buried under his books and papers.

'"Here it is!" he cried, pulling it out. He was so surprised and pleased with himself at finding it quickly that he did a little jig and almost upset his breakfast over the table. "Come and sit beside me on the bench while I read, Tashi," he invited.

'"Anyone who has already had such an exciting life as yours would be sure to have a very interesting future ahead of him."

'Well, I watched him read for a minute, and then suddenly he stopped smiling and covered his eyes with his hands.

'"Oh, Tashi," he said in a sorrowful voice.

'"What? What is it?"

'"Oh, Tashi, on the morning of your 10th birthday you are going to die!"

'"But that will be the day after tomorrow! Are you sure, Luk Ahed? I'm so healthy – look!" I jumped up and down and did one-arm push ups to show him I wasn't even breathing hard.

'Luk Ahed shook his head sadly. "I'm sorry, Tashi, but we can't argue with destiny."

'"There must be something we can do. Couldn't *you* put in a good word for me?"

'Luk Ahed laughed unhappily. "*I'm* not important enough for that, Tashi. No, once your name has been written in the Great Book of Fate, there is nothing . . . " He paused. "Except your name hasn't been entered in the Book yet, has it? And it won't be written in until New Year's Eve . . . in two days' time. And if on that evening you were to . . . "

'I was beginning to notice that Luk Ahed had a very annoying habit of not finishing his sentences. "If I were to *what*, Luk Ahed?"

'The fortune teller was feverishly looking through his sacred books. "The Gods like to enjoy a particular meal on New Year's Eve," he said. "Very simple, but special. Each God has his own favourite dishes. Now, if we were to serve our God of Long Life his own personal special meal, cooked to perfection . . . "

'"He might put me back in the Book of Life!" I finished his sentence.

'"Exactly."'

'So what are the special dishes?' asked Uncle Joe. 'Not crocodile, by any chance? Braised perhaps, with noodles?'

'No,' Tashi shook his head. 'Wild mushroom omelette with nightingale eggs. Speckled trout with wine and ginger. And a bowl of golden raspberries.'

'Gosh!' said Dad. 'Where would you get a nightingale egg? *Are* there any in your part of the world, Tashi?'

'Not that I knew of – I'd never seen any nests in our forests. For a moment I did feel low, I can tell you. It all seemed impossible. But then I thought of my friend, the raven. He *had* said, "Just whistle if you ever need my help." Remember when he was hurt after that terrible storm, Jack? The night Baba Yaga blew in? And I knew the children I had rescued from the war lord would gladly gather the mushrooms for me. And Lotus Blossom's mother had a pond at the bottom of her house where I was almost *sure* I'd seen speckled trout swimming. Maybe it wasn't impossible after all.

'So I hastily said goodbye to Luk Ahed and ran home to the mulberry tree where the raven sometimes perched. He flew down at my second whistle and when I told him about the dinner and the nightingale eggs, he said, "Give me your straw basket and I will be back with them tomorrow."

'The village children were very excited when I explained about the mushrooms.

'"We'll find enough for twenty Gods, Tashi," they shouted. Off they ran with their bags, clattering over the bridge into the fields and forest.

43

'Meanwhile, I hurried to Lotus Blossom's house. Her mother wasn't so happy to lose the beautiful speckled trout – they were her last three – but she gave a good-hearted smile as she scooped them out of her pond and handed them to me in a bowl of water.

'I raced back to the square where Luk Ahed stood, waving his hands. There was a great argument going on in the village about who would be the best people to cook the dishes. No one was listening to Luk Ahed, who was calling for order. Finally everyone agreed that Sixth Aunt Chow made the most delicious omelettes, but that Big Wu and his Younger Brother, Little Wu, should cook the fish.

'Next morning, cooking fires were set
up in the square so everyone could watch
and advise. The children were back before
noon with beautiful baskets overflowing
with four different kinds of mushrooms.
In the early afternoon the raven returned.
He looked quite bedraggled and tired,
but in the basket were a dozen perfect
nightingale eggs.

'Mrs Li brought out a bottle of her
prized wine to add to the fish and I left
them all busily chopping ginger roots and
celery and bamboo shoots.

'Now the hardest task lay ahead. In all
our province I had only ever seen one bush
of golden raspberries. And it belonged to
my enemy, the wicked Baron.'

'Oh, no!' cried Jack.

'Oh, yes!' said Tashi. 'I had brought my magic shoes with me but I decided not to put them on. As I walked slowly to his house I went over in my mind exactly *how* I would go about asking the Baron for a bowl of his berries.

'But I didn't have to ask. He had already heard the news and he was waiting for me with a fat smile on his face.

'"Well, Tashi," he gloated, "I hear that you are in need of some of my berries."

'"Yes, please."

'"Oh, you'll have to do much better than that." He shook a playful finger at me. "Something like this. Now, Tashi, say after me: Please, please most kindly, honourable and worthy Baron, could you give some berries to this miserable little worm Tashi, who stands before you?"

'I gritted my teeth and managed to force out the words, but the Baron pretended he couldn't hear and made me say it all over again. When I had finished, he thumped his fist on the table and shouted, "No, I couldn't! After all the trouble you have caused me, I'll be glad to be rid of you. Not a berry will you have."

'I was just leaving his house when Third Aunt called after me. She worked in the Baron's kitchen, remember, Jack? Well, she came close and whispered, "There *is* another bush of golden raspberries, Tashi. It belongs to the Old Witch who lives in the forest. But don't take any without asking her. The berries scream if anyone except the witch picks them."

'Oh dear, I didn't like the sound of that but what was I to do? It was the Old Witch's berries or none.

'This time I slipped my magic shoes on and I was in the forest in a few bounds. I found the Witch's cottage and there in the garden at the back of the house was a small raspberry bush. There were only a few golden berries on it but they looked round and juicy. I touched one gently and it gave a little scream.

'A door opened at once and a bony old
figure in a dusty black cloak came hobbling
down the path.

'"Who is meddling with my raspberry
bush?" she shrieked.

'She looked like a bunch of old broom
sticks strung together. She was even more
hideous than people had said. Her
blackened teeth were bared in a fierce growl
and her bristly chin was thrust out so far
in rage that her beak almost touched it.
I turned to run. I expected my magic shoes
would take me to safety in one bound, but
something in the way she stood there, alone
on the garden path, made me stop. Her
mouth puckered around her gums and her
eyes were sad. Come
to think of it, I had
never heard of
her harming
anyone.

'I took a deep breath and said, "I was
just looking at them, Granny, because
I have a great need of golden raspberries
at the moment."

'She cackled. "Oh, you have, have you?"
And she sat herself down on a bench. "Tell
me about it then."

'When I had finished, she pulled herself
up on my arm. She grinned at me, and with
her mouth no longer set in a growl and her
eyes sparkling with interest, she didn't look
nearly so scary. "Come on then," she said,
"we'll make a nice pot of tea and then you
can pick your berries. There aren't many
left but you'll find enough to fill a bowl,
I'm sure."

'You can imagine how joyfully I ran back with my basket of fruit. But when I reached the bridge by the Baron's house, he was standing there, blocking my way. His eyes bulged when he saw my berries and with a roar of rage he charged towards me and knocked the basket up in the air and into the river. I hung over the railing and watched in despair as the berries bobbed away downstream.

'"How are you going to prepare your wonderful meal now, eh, clever Tashi?" the Baron sneered.

'I struggled to hold in my bitter feelings and faced him calmly. "We'll prepare the rest of the meal and I will take it to the mountain top, to the *Gods*, together with a note explaining that the delicious golden raspberries are missing because the wicked Baron, *YOU*, knocked them into the river."

'The Baron's jaw dropped and his mouth opened and closed. "That won't be necessary, my boy. Couldn't you see that I was just having a joke with you?"

'I folded my arms and said nothing
while the Baron pleaded with me to take all
the golden raspberries I needed.

'Finally, I shook my finger at him. "Oh,
you will have to do much better than that.
Now, Baron, say after me: Please, please
most kindly, honourable and worthy Tashi,
could you take the berries of this miserable
worm of a Baron, who stands before you?"

'The Baron gritted his teeth and forced
out the words. He even tried to smile as
I picked his fruit. I thanked him politely
for holding the basket for me.

'It was late afternoon by the time I got back to the village and everything was ready. A wonderful omelette filled with delicate flavoursome mushrooms lay on some vine leaves upon my mother's best platter. My mouth watered as I lifted the lid from the dish of speckled trout in wine and ginger and pickled vegetables that only Big Wu and Little Wu knew how to prepare. We washed the raspberries in fresh spring water, dried them and placed them gently in a moss-lined basket.

'Luk Ahed and I carried two baskets
each and when we reached the mountain
top, we spread out a gleaming white linen
tablecloth and set out the meal. It was
perfect.

'When it was nearly midnight we hid
behind a tree and waited. On the stroke of
twelve we were dazzled by a blinding silver
light. We blinked against the light, closing
our eyes for just a moment, but when we
could see again the cloth was bare.

'Luk Ahed and I ran all the way back down the mountain and hurried to his house to see if my horoscope had changed. Luk Ahed peered at the chart, his brow wrinkling deeper with every second. I was holding my breath, and began to feel faint. If he didn't answer soon, I thought I might fall over and die right where I stood.

'"Tashi, the bad news is that all our work preparing that magnificent meal was for nothing."

'"!!!???!!!??"

'Then he smiled guiltily, bowing his head. "The *good* news is that you didn't need to do any of it. Look, here where I read *10th* birthday, it was really your *100th* birthday. You see, a little bit of breakfast pancake was covering the last zero."

'We stared at each other for a moment and began to laugh.

'"Let's not tell the village," said Luk Ahed. "They might be a little bit cross with me."'

The family looked at Tashi with their

mouths open. Uncle Joe's was still full of ghost pie, and a dollop fell out onto the table.

Jack cleared his throat. 'So how do you think you'll feel when you are nearly one hundred and you know you're going to die?'

'Oh,' Tashi waved airily, 'if I'm not quite ready, I'll just prepare another perfect meal for the God of Long Life.'

'Here's to a l-o-n-g friendship then,' said Uncle Joe, raising his glass of wine. They all clinked glasses and wished each other well. Then Uncle Joe added, 'You know, Tashi, that ghost pie really was excellent. It's given me a lot of energy. I think I'll go and stretch my legs after that long meal.' And he rubbed his hands together with excitement.

'It only lasts for three days!' Tashi called out, but Uncle Joe had already walked through the kitchen wall, and was gone.

'Great way to travel,' he yelled from the garden. 'See you soon!' And they heard him humming the old song, *'No walls can keep me in, no woman can tie me down, no jail can hold me now, da dum da dum da dum . . .'*

# Tashi
## and the
# HAUNTED
# HOUSE

written by
**Anna Fienberg**
and
**Barbara Fienberg**
•

illustrated by
**Kim Gamble**

**ALLEN&UNWIN**

'Well, look who's here!' cried Uncle Joe, as he spied Tashi strolling up the garden path. He leapt from his chair and sprinted across the lawn.

'I was just thinking about you, my boy! There's someone *special* I want you to meet.' Uncle Joe's eyes were dancing and he kept fidgeting in his pockets and sucking at his moustache while he shot quick, shy glances around the garden.

The rest of the family were busy digging
and planting for Spring. Tashi saw a new
herb patch near the steps and Jack was
potting a tomato plant. Suddenly, a dark-
haired lady stepped out from behind the
box hedge.

'Primrose! There you are!' Joe cried
proudly.

Primrose smiled and put out her hand
for Tashi to shake.

Uncle Joe looked from one to the other, beaming. 'I met Primrose up north, you see, when I was camping by a river *jumping* with barramundi.'

'Oh, so that's where you went after you walked through the kitchen wall?' Tashi asked with interest.

'Yes, yes, and I told dear Primrose all about your ghostly adventures, Tashi, as she and I fished by the river in the moonlight and fell hopelessly in love. Do you know, Primrose is not only the best angler I've met in my time but she's also an amazing musician. A percussionist!'

'I just tap on things,' Primrose said mildly. She picked up a teaspoon lying on the table and tapped lightly on the glasses and jugs, making a tinkling little tune.

'What I like best, though,' Primrose said confidingly to Tashi, 'is to make sounds with things from the natural world. I'm always searching for different, curious things to tap.'

Just then Jack came over, his hands black with dirt. 'Do you know, Tashi, Primrose can make scary, ghostly noises, just with bottles and wood and things? If you close your eyes and listen, you'd swear a million ghosts were breathing down your neck!'

Tashi nodded as Mum began pouring lemonade for everyone.

'You remind me of my cousin, Lotus Blossom,' Tashi said to Primrose.

'What, the one who keeps disappearing?' Joe asked in alarm.

'Yes,' said Tashi. 'But not because of that. No, once Lotus Blossom and I were in a situation of terrible danger and we needed to summon up the sound of ghostly voices. She did it very well.'

'Ghosts, eh Tashi?' put in Dad, as he peeled off his gardening gloves. He nudged Joe happily.

'So, tell us about Lotus Blossom,' said
Primrose. 'Was she a percussionist like me?'

'No,' grinned Tashi. 'She was a pest. But
she did have some good ideas. Especially
when it came to the haunted house.'

Everyone watched as Tashi took a sip
of lemonade.

'Go on,' urged Mum.

'Well, it was like this. Ever since I can
remember, the ghost house has been there,

crouching in the gloomiest part of the forest. No one from our village had set foot in that place, ever. Well, not for thirty years, anyway. Not since something dreadful happened to the old couple who used to live there. We children could never find out exactly *what* happened. The grown-ups would look frightened when we asked and say, "We don't want to talk about it."'

Jack snorted. 'That'd be right.'

'Sometimes we'd scare ourselves sick by
running past the house or dare each other
to go right up the path. So far only Ah Chu
and I had actually dared to creep up and
knock on the door.

'Then one winter's evening, Ah Chu's
father caught up with us on the way home.
He'd been in the forest burning charcoal
and his hands were black with soot. They
looked a bit like yours, Jack! But I still
remember how they trembled when he
shook my shoulder.

'Don't go near the ghost house,' he
warned. 'I've just seen a light flickering in
the window. Who knows *what* is prowling
around in there!'

'Wah! He hurried on his way and we
went on making our dam in the creek.
Neither of us said a word, but you can be
sure we were both thinking about the ghost
house, and the strange light burning there.
We knew that the next day we would just
have to go and see for ourselves.

'Darkness comes early in those winter
afternoons so we hurried through the
forest, our hearts thumping at every bird
calling, or branch snapping.'

*Cra-ack!* Primrose broke a stick over
her knee and Dad nearly fell off his chair.

'Sorry,' she whispered. 'I was just adding
sound effects.'

'Well, Lotus Blossom came with us that afternoon because she hates to miss out on anything and, besides, she said she would tell Ah Chu's father if we didn't let her come. Off she went running as fast as she could through the trees, far ahead of us, until we lost sight of her. But when we drew near the house, wasn't she leaning against a tree, panting, with a stitch in her side?

'I couldn't help laughing, but then Ah Chu said he had to stop too, because he had a pebble in his shoe and a sore foot. So I had to go up the path alone.

'I crept along slowly, over patches of damp green moss and through vines as thick as your fist. The house rose up before me, dark and full of shadows – it was like an animal in its lair, half hidden by the webbed shade of the trees.

'The latch lifted stiffly in my clammy hand and the door creaked open. "Come *on*!" I called over my shoulder and waited while Ah Chu and Lotus Blossom pushed each other up the path.

'I went first. It was black as a bat's cave inside, and smelled of mould. The further in we crept, the colder it grew. It was like walking into a grave. Something sticky and soft brushed against my face – *ugh!* – spiderwebs! When my eyes grew used to the dark I saw dust hanging in long strands from the rafters like ghostly grey ribbons.

'Then Lotus Blossom yelped suddenly as her foot went through a rotten floorboard. Wah! She nearly fell through the hole!

'"I thought something grabbed my ankle," she whispered.

'We clung together, listening to the silence. Even our breathing was loud. And then came the sound of a careful footstep from the room above our head. Ah Chu moaned.

'I stepped forward. "Is anybody there?" I called.

'We heard a creak and a flurry of steps and then *crash*! A great beam that had been holding up the ceiling came hurtling down, landing in a huge cloud of dust just millimetres from my nose.

'We all reached the door at once, so for a moment no one could get out. Ah Chu is quite plump and almost filled the doorway by himself but he and Lotus Blossom finally pushed through and were down the path like pellets out of a peashooter.

'I was about to follow, I can tell you – '

'Quick, quick, didn't you get out of
there?' cried Jack.

'Well, I looked back, just for a second,
and there, sprawled among the rubble
of the fallen ceiling was a young woman.
She lifted her head and groaned, so I raced
back to her.

'"Are you hurt? Have you broken
something?"

'She tried to stand up. "My ankle aches terribly," she whispered. "Oh, I knew the floor was rotten but I was so frightened. I thought you were someone sent by my cousin to take me back." She looked at me closely. "You're not, are you?"

'"No, I'm Tashi. I don't even know your cousin. Why are you so scared of him?"

'"When my mother and father died, my cousin Bu Li moved in. I always hated him – he's so much older than me and strong as an ox. He kept me locked in the house from morning till night, dyeing his silk. "You'll stay here and be my slave," he bellowed at me everyday, "until you tell me where you've hidden that emerald ring your mother left you." But I *wouldn't*! She told me before she died that I could use it to start a new life, and that is what I'm going to do."

'Ning Jing, for that was her name, pulled out a little bag hanging on a string around

82

her neck. I looked at the ring respectfully. It was the first emerald I'd ever seen; it was green like the moss outside, green like a cat's eyes in the dark.

'I noticed that Ning Jing was rubbing her ankle, so I said, "If your leg is hurting, why don't you stay here tonight and rest it?"

'Ning Jing nodded. "But I would need some food, Tashi. I have only this one fish cake left."

'"Tomorrow, straight after school, I'll bring you some more food from home. And then you can go on your way to the city."

'I had gone down the path only a little way when Ah Chu and Lotus Blossom popped out of some bushes to join me. We stopped and sat for a while in the gathering dusk as they peppered me with questions. I told them all about Ning Jing and her horrible cousin, and the emerald winking like a cat's eye.

'"Thank the Gods of Long Life," sighed Lotus Blossom. "I'm so glad that the ghost was instead a Ning Jing!"

'They both promised that they would come with me the next day with the food.

'Never was a day so long. As soon as school was over we raced home to collect the food. Ah Chu, who always took a great interest in eating, raided his mother's kitchen so well that he took an age to arrive, laden down with heavy baskets. And that is why, of course, he needed to sit down for a little rest on the way to the house while we went on ahead. And that's how he came to hear three men blundering about in the forest. He pricked up his ears like a fox when he heard the name Ning Jing.

'"Demon of a woman!" hissed the man with the long thin beard. "That Ning Jing – her mother was just like her. Stubborn as a mule, tricky as a weasel. Now which way did she go?"

'"There's no track here, no sign of her at all."

'"Well if you'd been keeping your eyes peeled instead of picking berries and stuffing yourself, we wouldn't have lost her!"

'When Ah Chu had heard enough, he stood up quietly and trickled off through the trees.

'Bursting into the ghost house, he cried, "Three men are looking for Ning Jing in the forest."

'"Does one man have a long straggly beard?" asked Ning Jing. When Ah Chu told her, she buried her face in her hands. "I can't fight my cousin any more," she murmured through her fingers. "Oh what will I do, Tashi?"

'She looked straight at me then, and so did the others. I was just beginning to feel a little bit annoyed about people always asking me that question, when I had an idea.

'"Don't worry," I said to Ning Jing.
"I've just thought of a plan. Ah Chu, you
hurry back to where you saw the men.
Tell them you've seen a young woman –
a stranger in the forest – and that she's
staying the night in an old empty house
close by. Don't forget to mention that the
house is haunted, and something dreadful
once happened there."

'Then I told Lotus Blossom that her job
was to follow Ah Chu, but to stay hidden
from the men. "You've got to make sure
that they're all thinking about ghosts by the
time they reach this house."

'"How?" she asked.'

'By making ghostly noises!' cried
Primrose suddenly. And she blew into the
empty lemonade bottle on the garden table,
making a low wheezy moan.

'That's it, my clever one!' cried Uncle
Joe, squeezing her arm.

'You've got it!' agreed Tashi. 'I told
Lotus Blossom I didn't know quite how
she'd do it, but I knew she'd think of
something.

'Well, Ah Chu quickly found the men
in the forest as they were still standing
there arguing.

'"Take us to the girl then, young fellow," said Cousin Bu Li, "and you'll have a little something for your trouble." Turning to his men he laughed, "And he'll get a fist in the belly if he doesn't!"

'"Ooh, sir, I don't know if I can, sir," shuddered Ah Chu, making his hands tremble. "That old house is haunted, ever since two people were murdered there... hung by their necks from the rafters!"

'"Haunted eh?" cousin Bu Li crowed. "A fine place she's chosen to hide. Why, she'll be glad to see us!"

'But Ah Chu noticed how pale he'd suddenly become.

'As they moved through the forest, the men grew quiet and jumpy. Suddenly they heard a low wailing and whistling like a whipping autumn wind. They stopped and peered around. But not a leaf moved in the stillness. Cousin Bu Li shivered. "Just a bird," he muttered, and moved on.

'A minute passed and now there came thin whooshing sounds like a hundred Samurai swords swiping at the air. Then a tremendous rattling noise of thunder made the men hold their hands to their ears, but the sky above them was clear and still as a piece of blue silk. A blood-curdling shriek – like a man having his throat cut from ear to ear – rushed the men through the forest, clutching onto each other's coats as they went.

'When they arrived at the path leading
to the house, Cousin Bu Li needed all his
promises of gold to urge the men on.

'"Ning Jing!" he shouted. "Come out at
once or you'll be sorry for the rest of your
short and miserable life!"

'There was no sound.

'The men edged into the house. They tasted the damp and the dust. They peered through the dark and the cobwebs. Then a deep shuddery wailing started and the men looked up to see a gaping black hole in the ceiling. The wail poured out of the darkness, filling the room like a river rushing into the sea.

'The two men turned and fled. Only cousin Bu Li stood his ground. Then the hairs on his neck stiffened.

'A light appeared, shining up into the
hole in the ceiling. It lit up a ghastly sight:
Ning Jing's headless body (he knew it was
Ning Jing because that was her dress with
the blue peacock on the front) and it was
swinging from an iron hook. A sob drew
his horrified gaze to an old chest in the
corner. Resting on the top of the chest was
... her head. The eyes in the head wept and

the mouth sobbed, "Oh, cousin, why did you drive me to my death?"

'Cousin Bu Li screamed and raced for the door. He bolted out of the house and ran so fast through the forest that he caught up with his men, passed them in a flash and left them far behind. He never went near that forest again for as long as he lived.

'Meanwhile, I wriggled out of Ning Jing's dress. You see, she was taller than me so the collar of her dress had covered my head. Ah Chu and Lotus Blossom, who had arrived back a few minutes before, helped me down and Ning Jing came out from behind the chest. She and her head skipped over to join us.

'"Oh, Tashi, that was wonderful. I'll never forget Cousin Bu Li's face when he looked up and saw – what he thought he saw!"

'Lotus Blossom was really cross. She said it was all very well for us, but she and Ah Chu hadn't heard about the plan and they'd had a nasty shock when they saw that swinging body and talking head. She shivered, saying the next time I had a clever idea I needn't bother to invite her along.

'"Well, who invited *you*?" I said, and she gave me a good pinch on the arm!

'Later, as we were enjoying a little snack of Ah Chu's food, I said to Ning Jing, "It was strange that you happened to be in the haunted house the very day we came."

'"Not so strange," said Ning Jing. "This house once belonged to my grandparents."

'"It did?" we cried. "What happened to them?"

'"What? What?"

'Ning Jing looked thoughtful. "I think that is something you should ask your parents."

Tashi sat back in his chair and grinned at Jack. 'And that was all we were ever able to find out.'

Jack said disgustedly, 'All grown-ups are the same, even the young ones. They never tell you anything.'

'Some do. Percussionists do,' argued Primrose. 'For example, I could tell you what Lotus Blossom used to make that whistling wind sound, the whipping Samuari swords, or the rattle like thunder.'

'Lotus Blossom probably told Tashi everything already,' protested Jack.

Tashi leaned forward and tapped his glass. 'No, she didn't, Jack. We had quite an argument, actually. I suppose she was still mad with me about the fright she got.' Tashi grinned into his lemonade. 'So, Primrose, how did she do it?'

'Well, come down into the garden and I'll show you. Now, let's see, what'll we need? Some small branches for whipping swords, I think, and pebbles to turn in a basin...'

But Jack and Tashi had already leapt up and dashed off across the lawn. Blood-curdling shrieks were heard as they disappeared amongst the trees.

Jack burst into the kitchen on Monday afternoon. 'Guess what happened at school today!'

'What?' cried Mum and Uncle Joe and Primrose, who stopped playing the conga drums to listen.

'Our class was in the assembly hall and we were doing a stomping dance when suddenly the stage floor fell in beneath us –'

'Batter the barramundi, was anyone hurt?' asked Uncle Joe.

'No,' replied Jack. 'Mrs Fitzpatrick leapt across the stage and saved Angus Figment who was right on the edge of this great ginormous hole. All the teachers gathered around and asked why wasn't there *ever* enough money for public schools and now they'd have to come up with *another* amazing idea for fund-raising to fix the floor, when Tashi stepped in –'

'Ho ho!' cried Dad, who'd just come in the door.

'Yes, and Tashi said, really quietly, you know how he is, that back in the old country he'd raised enough money to build a whole new school! When all the teachers asked "How?" Tashi said, "Well, it was like this – "'

Suddenly the kitchen was filled with a drum roll from the congas.

'Thank you, Primrose,' Mum said, holding her head. 'Perhaps we can leave that for the end of the story, dear.'

'Yes, let's,' agreed Primrose enthusiastically, 'or better, what about one super duper roll for the climax, and a soft, furry one for the finish?'

Mum nodded weakly. 'So, how did he do it, Jack?'

'Well, Tashi said everybody had known for ages that something would have to be done about their village school-house. The walls were all wrinkled and powdery with dry rot. Sometimes, the children could hear rustling sounds of white ants chewing at the wood.

'But it was an awful shock when suddenly one morning – luckily while everyone was outside – the large roof beam cracked and sagged. Just a minute later the whole building slowly collapsed, and the walls quietly fell in like buckling knees.'

'BOOF! BANG! BOOM!' went the drums.

'That's not the climax!' Mum protested. 'And didn't Jack say *quietly*?'

'Sorry,' grinned Primrose. 'I couldn't resist. That was an exclamation mark.'

'Well, anyway,' Jack went on, 'teacher Pang and the children stood open-mouthed at the sight of their school-house turned in one moment into a pile of dust and rubble.

'"What luck!" cried Ah Chu (who hated spelling tests). "No more school! Who's coming fishing?"

'"Not me," said Tashi. "Fishing is one thing, holidays are fun, but just think, to have no school at all, ever! It would be so boring."

'A meeting was called in the village to try to find a way of building a new school. A few people brought along some timber and roof tiles and put them in the middle of the square, but there was not nearly enough. No one had any money to spare, as usual.

'And then, two strangers wandered into the square. They were a mysterious-looking pair. Their clothes didn't quite fit and although their large hats hid most of their faces, Tashi thought he saw a pair of yellow tusks as one smiled. And there, as one stranger turned to point Tashi out to the other, Tashi saw a a tail poking out from under his coat! *Demons!*'

'Oh, *those* thick-headed thugs!' cried
Dad. 'Remember when they poured spiders
and snakes onto Tashi and he tricked them,
jumping into that old Dragon's Blood tree?'

'That's right,' said Jack. 'And that's why
Tashi was especially nervous now. Because
demons are always dangerous, but angry
demons with revenge in their hearts are
diabolical. And now what on earth were
they doing in his village square?

'The demons stood still as stones,
listening to all the talk and wild
suggestions. But finally one of them
boomed over all the voices.

'"No, no, what you must do is give us a race around the village! We'll race one of these children." He pointed a claw-finger at Tashi. "This little dillblot here, for instance. If he wins, we'll give you all the bricks and timber for a new school."

'"And if he loses?"

'"If he loses, he'll be ours to do with as we will." And behind his hand he gave a laugh that cracked with demon spite.

'Oh *NO*!" cried the villagers and Tashi's family. Especially Tashi's family.

'But the Baron pushed through the crowd. "I think that's an excellent idea. Who would like to wager that Tashi wins?"

'The villagers were so eager to show their faith in Tashi that they all put their hands up before they realised they had been tricked into agreeing.

'"That's settled then," the Baron smiled nastily. The demons poked each other in the ribs and sniggered.

'*He's* the dillblot!' exploded Dad. 'That Baron could buy ten new school-houses for the village and not even dent his mountain of money. But would he? Never!'

'"First I'll go home and get my running shoes," Tashi told the villagers. "I'll be back here in one hour," he called over his shoulder.

'"Yes, so will we," hissed the demons and Tashi spied fat drops of drool sliding out from beneath their tusks.

'"Now where are they off to?" Tashi wondered as the family hurried home with him, begging him not to take part in the race.

'"Don't worry," Tashi comforted his mother. "I'll be quite safe with these on." And he pulled his magic dancing shoes out of the playbox in his room. "In just a few seconds I can leap across fields and forests with these."

'While he was putting on his shoes, he told the family that they were right to be suspicious about the strangers; they were the two demons who had tortured him with spiders and snakes once before. The family was horrified.

'"I thought there was something odd when they called you a dillblot," said Tashi's father. "What does that mean? I said to myself. Now I know – *demons* eh? They're famous for their poor vocabulary.

'Now Tashi, my boy, if you must do this, please test your shoes one last time to be sure that the magic is still working."

'Tashi agreed, and when they returned to the square all the villagers were waiting.

'The Wicked Baron raised his silk handkerchief. "Let the race begin!"

'The demons bared their tusks and their terrible eyes spun and blazed but at the

word "GO!" they shot off towards the
forest. Tashi had never seen anyone run
so fast.

'He waited until he felt his feet tingle and then he was away. In two minutes he had flashed past the astonished demons. He'd just reached the half-way mark when, as his foot touched the ground for the next step, a loop of tough vine closed around it and he was jerked upside down – he found himself swinging from a tall tree. Hadn't he stepped right into a Tashi-trap the demons had prepared for him? *Wah!*

'In the distance he could see the demons coming nearer. He struggled and rocked himself in anguish. He knew what they would do to him once they found him dangling helplessly from a tree. He jerked and twisted but the vine held him fast.

'And then he noticed that he *was* swinging a little. He arched his back and drew up his knees. His swings grew wider and higher. Just a little more and he was able to grab at a branch of a tree and pull himself up.

'There were crashing sounds down in the
bushes below and two hot and dripping
demons went panting past. Tashi sat astride
the branch and slipped the vine over his
ankle. Then he scrambled down to the
ground and set off again.

'He was just catching up with the demons when he noticed that a mist was rolling in through the trees. In an instant it had thickened so much that the demons ahead disappeared from sight. Tashi crept on slowly, feeling his way, bumping into trees. The fog was cold like a rain cloud, and tasted stale and wet on his lips. He kept blinking against the grey light but it was as if a bandage had been pulled tight over his eyes. He jumped when he heard demon voices right beside him.

'"I can't believe you let the misty stuff
out of the bottle in *front* of us instead of
behind us! How did you reckon we'd find
our way through this fog-thing?" shouted
the first demon.

'"I didn't think," whined the second.
"Couldn't you get it back in again?"

'"You can't put the fog-thing back into
a bottle once it's out, you dillblot. Don't
you know anything? At least Tashi won't be
able to see either. We'll just have to sit
here until it blows away. *Dill*blot."

'Tashi moved on carefully until his outstretched hands met a fence. He followed the fence around until he came to a familiar gatepost. "I know this gate!" he thought joyfully. "It belongs to Granny White Eyes."

'Granny White Eyes was so called because she could not see. Tashi and the other children of the village loved going to her house because she always had an interesting story to tell. Her brother had been a sailor and she'd accompanied him on many trips to exotic parts of the world.

'Tashi crawled up the garden path and knocked on the door. Lotus Blossom opened it.

'"Hello, Tashi. Oh, Granny White Eyes," she called into the darkness behind her, "it's Tashi come to see you!"

'An old woman came slowly to the door. "Tashi! Come in, what a lovely surprise. I wasn't expecting you today."

'"Well, this isn't exactly a visit," said Tashi. "It's like this," and he told her about the school-house and the demons and the race. "So," he finished, "I was wondering if you could lead me back to the village, Granny White Eyes."

"Of course I can," she laughed. "Mist or no mist, it makes no difference to me. I know every twist and turn in the path as well as my own kitchen. Come on."

'Tashi held on tight to her coat and they set off at a brisk pace through the blinding mist. Just before they reached the village, the fog cleared and Tashi stopped.

'"I can see now. Granny White Eyes, would you like to run like the wind with me on my magic shoes?"

'Her face creased into a wide smile. "Tashi, I would."

'Tashi knelt down and she climbed onto his shoulders. Granny screamed with delight as they sped over the ground.

'"Oh Tashi, I never thought I would fly through the air like this. It's wonderful."

'And didn't the village cheer as they zipped into the square? The people crowded around to hear what happened, nudging each other, trying to get close to Tashi. All except the Baron, of course.

He went home.

'A bedraggled pair of demons finally found their way back to the village. They cursed and spat and "dillblotted" every-where, but by late afternoon they had unloaded a cartful of bricks and tiles in the village square.

'And that is why the new school-house has Tashi's name over the door, and why sometimes, on cold Monday mornings, (especially when there's a spelling test) his friend Ah Chu mutters, "What a clever Tashi!"

Mum sighed happily, then jumped as if she'd been shot.

'BOOF! BANG! BOOM!' went the drums.

'You were a bit late weren't you, Primrose?' said Mum crossly.

'A little,' admitted Primrose. 'I got caught up in the story and forgot.'

'Well, I haven't forgotten about that stage floor at your school, Jack,' said Dad, shaking his head. 'Has Tashi spotted any helpful demons in this suburb?'

'Not yet,' said Jack. 'But he's keeping his eye out.'

# Tashi

## and the
# ROYAL
# TOMB

written by
**Anna Fienberg**
and
**Barbara Fienberg**
·

illustrated by
**Kim Gamble**

**ALLEN&UNWIN**

When Jack and Tashi raced to the
classroom one Monday morning, they
screeched to a halt at the door. Was this
the right room? The walls were splashed
with paintings of pyramids, mummies lying
in tombs, strange writing made up of little
pictures. From the ceiling hung masks of
jackals and fierce-looking kings, and the
heavy air smelled sweet, musty like Jack's
jumper drawer where Mum kept a bag
of dried flowers.

'Look!' cried Jack, pointing to gold pots of incense burning on the windowsill. The smoke hung in a curtain above their heads, mysterious, exotic.

'In ancient Egypt,' Mrs Hall, the teacher, said grandly as she swept into the room, 'pharaohs were buried in mansions of eternity –'

'Pyramids!' called out Angus Figment.

'Magnificent tombs,' agreed Mrs Hall, 'with burial chambers inside, filled with everything the king might need for the afterlife –'

'And the pharaohs were made into mummies before they were buried,' put in Angus Figment. 'All their livers and stomachs and whatnot were pulled out first, and then the bodies were washed with palm wine and covered with salt, and the priests used to burn incense to take away the pong because all the gasses in the bodies must have stunk like crazy –'

'Thank you, Angus,' said Mrs Hall.

Angus looked around the room happily.
He'd been mad on ancient Egypt since
kindergarten, and knew all sorts of
interesting details about burial methods
and coffins. His mother had grown
worried about him in Year 1 when he'd
talked about embalming the cat, but the
school counsellor told her Angus just had
a terrific imagination, and soon he'd move
on to other things. His mother (and the
cat) were still waiting.

'The Viking kings used to have their
slaves and warriors buried with them,'
Jack put in.

'Back in my country,' Tashi said quietly,
'we had tombs, too.'

Mrs Hall looked at him. Her eyes were
round with interest. 'Did you ever see
any?' she asked. 'Were there any ancient
burial sites near your village?'

'Oh yes,' said Tashi. 'A royal tomb was discovered, and I was nearly buried alive in it!'

'Like a Viking slave!' cried Jack. 'Tell us what happened!'

'Yes,' said Mrs Hall, eagerly pulling up her chair near Tashi. 'Please do.'

'Well,' said Tashi, 'it was like this. Big Uncle had decided he needed a new well. You see, he lived quite far from the village and his wife was tired of having to trudge all that way for their water. So he asked our family to help him dig a new well on his land. Of course, when I told the teacher that I had to miss a day at school, Ah Chu and Lotus Blossom wanted to come too and help.'

'And did they?' asked Jack enviously.

'Oh yes,' said Tashi. 'You know how Lotus Blossom always gets her way. It was fun at first. We poked about in the soil, the men carried away buckets of stones and we built castles with them – that is until Ah Chu sat on them to eat his lunch.

'But the really thrilling part came when the men dug deeper and began to scoop out marvellous treasures, one after the other.

'Ah Chu found a bowl decorated with a golden dragon and then, right next to me, Lotus Blossom gently brushed the soil away from a beautiful bronze tiger.

'When Big Uncle himself uncovered a full-sized terracotta warrior, he told everybody to stop work.

"'This looks like an important find,'" he said. "We'll have to send word to the museum in the city and let the archaeologists come out and see it."

'Well, I was disappointed – I'd been hoping to find some exciting thing, too. I stepped over to look more closely at the warrior's battle robe and touch the scarf around his neck. I examined the warrior's face, and looked into his eyes. And then, it was spooky, everything around me went still for a moment, like when the wind stops in the middle of a storm. I could have sworn the warrior was holding my gaze. There was a circle of silence around us, with just our eyes speaking.

'"What?" I whispered, and perhaps I heard a faint sound. But now Big Uncle and my father bustled up to move everyone away from the digging and to fence it off with a rope.

'Just then, too late, the Baron came charging up the hill. "What's this I hear?" he shouted. "I don't believe it! A burial site found here on your land?"'

'Typical,' groaned Jack. 'That selfish money-bags ruins everything!'

'Yes,' agreed Tashi. 'He's got snake oil running in his veins instead of blood, I bet. Well, he blustered "Why wasn't I told?" and "This will be worth a fortune! To think, the number of times I've crossed this very field, never suspecting what was lying under my feet."

'"Well, if it is a King's tomb," my father said gravely, "the government will claim it, you know. It won't be *our* fortune."

'The Baron looked at us with contempt. "These people simply have no idea," I heard him mutter to himself. No one was supposed to go near the dig until the experts from the city arrived, but the Baron jumped the rope fence and went in to take a good look around.

'Big Uncle gloomily went searching for another spot for his well and I *tried* to be patient. But I kept picturing the warrior's eyes and how he seemed to be speaking to me.

'On the fifth day, the team of archaeologists from the city arrived, and they were very excited. "This is a small tomb," Director Han explained, "but very important."

'Teacher Pang had brought the whole school up to hear the verdict and nearly everyone else in the village had followed. They crowded closer to listen.

'"We'll dig out this fallen soil and restore the walls and the brick floor of the tomb, and then we'll put all the warriors and their swords and things back just as they were," Director Han told them. "Unfortunately, as often happens, it seems the King's burial chamber itself has been robbed and destroyed, but there are still many precious things here in the outer tomb. I'm sure we will find more."

'Teacher Pang was excited. "Imagine, children, we'll be able to step into the tomb and go back two thousand years in time!"'

'How *marvellous*!' Mrs Hall couldn't
help exclaiming, knocking Tashi's pencils
off the desk. 'Do you know, when the
Great Pyramid was opened up, hot air
rushed out and an Egyptian archaeologist
said, "I smelt incense . . . I smelt time . . .
I smelt centuries . . . I smelt history itself!"
*Imagine*, children, what that would
be like!'

'I'm going to be an archaeologist when
I grow up,' said Angus Figment.

'Well,' Tashi went on, 'several people from the village were given jobs digging, and I begged so hard that Director Han said I could be in charge of the teapot for the men's refreshments. This meant I often passed by my particular warrior, and always I felt the soldier's eyes were following me. But there was so much to see and do, with amazing finds each day: strange coins, weapons, buckles of gold, and even a terracotta chariot and horses.

'So it wasn't until the dig was almost finished that I felt the pull of the warrior's gaze. Glancing around to make sure no one was near, I knelt down and whispered to him, "What is it?"

'To my amazement, I heard a faint voice: "*Help me.*"

'"How? How can I help?"

'"My wife has just been unearthed over there by the chariot. I will never be able to rest until we are standing side by side."

'"That can't be," I told him, "there aren't any women in the tomb."

'"My wife dressed as a warrior. No one suspected she was a girl. We were part of the King's guard, and after I discovered her secret I fell in love with her and we married. Could you bring her over to my side so that we will have at least this short time together?"

'I thought for a moment. It was fine in the day when all the workers were talking and singing around me, but I must say I didn't like the idea of coming to the tomb at night. Still, I heard myself saying, "All right, I'll come back after dark when everyone has gone home."

'I was really glad there weren't any ghosts about when I arrived at the dig that night. I had great trouble finding the warrior-wife, even with the lantern I'd brought, and still more trouble lifting her into a wheelbarrow that luckily was lying about.

'I saw the warrior's eyes glow with joy.
I was just unloading her beside him when
I heard voices. So I ducked down behind
a rock and waited.

'The light of the lanterns lit the faces
of three men as they drew near. I gave a
little snort of disgust. Of course! Who else
would it be, to come robbing the tomb?
The beastly Baron. He and two of his men
were arguing. The men were saying that it
was unlucky and dangerous to steal from
a tomb.

'"Nonsense!" snapped the Baron. "No one has even seen these golden drinking vessels yet, so they won't even know they're missing."

'The men very reluctantly agreed to do what he wanted and they moved closer to where I was hiding. I jumped back and stumbled on a stone. Wah!

'In the blink of an eye the men seized
me, and just as I'd said a moment before
about *him*, the Baron growled, "Who else
would it be? Why is this boy always
under my feet plaguing me?"

'"What do you want us to do with him?"
asked the fiercer of the two men.

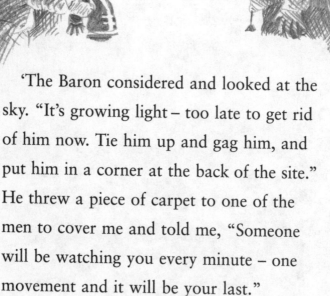

'The Baron considered and looked at the
sky. "It's growing light – too late to get rid
of him now. Tie him up and gag him, and
put him in a corner at the back of the site."
He threw a piece of carpet to one of the
men to cover me and told me, "Someone
will be watching you every minute – one
movement and it will be your last."

'Then the men bundled me up and stashed me away as if I were nothing but a bag of old rags.

'"We'll have to leave the sack of golden goblets here for now," I heard one of them say. "Put them back under the warrior's feet. Now let's go. That Han always arrives at first light, and the diggers from the village won't be far behind."

'The morning crept on. The sun rose
high in the sky, glaring down on me. My
throat was so dry it felt as if it had been
scraped with sandpaper. My tongue grew
huge in my mouth. I could hardly breathe
under the heavy dusty carpet and although
I sneezed several times, no one heard
because of the tight gag over my mouth.
The cords around my wrist cut into my
skin. And all the time, when I wasn't
dreaming of water, oh beautiful water,
I was thinking, just how were they going to
"get rid of me"?

'My brain was hurting with trying to think of a way to raise help. And how could I think properly when there was this strange voice in my head telling me to "Push back, push back . . ." What did it mean? The voice was inside me, but it wasn't my own. It was as if someone else had got hold of my head and was telling me what to think.

'I could hear Lotus Blossom and Ah Chu, sometimes passing so close, calling my name, asking if anyone had seen Tashi.

'"It's not like Tashi to just disappear, leaving us with no tea," Big Uncle grumbled.

'By late afternoon, only the last two warriors needed to be moved back into place. The Baron's men made sure they were there on the spot. "It will be dark in a moment," they pointed out to Director Han. "Perhaps it would be better to start throwing the rubbish over the cliff and leave the two warriors till morning? We don't want to drop them because we can't see what we're doing."

'"Yes, I agree," Director Han nodded, "and we'll cover the rubbish up with soil before we go."

'"*Waaah!*" I screamed silently under
my carpet. "They'll dump me over the cliff
with the rubbish. If I don't die from the
fall, I'll be buried alive under the soil."
And all the time the strange voice in
my head was growing stronger – it was
shouting now, "Push *back*!" I could no
longer ignore it. I focussed my mind on
the voice. And as I listened, a picture came
into my mind. I saw the eyes of my
warrior – they were wide and staring at a
small ledge jutting out of the wall behind
me. "*Push back*," he said to me urgently.

'I pushed back into the wall of the tomb.
Something moved behind me. A door was
opening in the thick stone wall. There was
nothing to hang onto and I fell backwards
down a flight of steps into the darkness
of a small room.

'By the dim light coming from the open door above, I could see that I had fallen down into the King's secret burial chamber. I saw an open coffin, and inside lay a skeleton in a magnificent jade burial suit. My heart leapt, but there was no time to look further. I glanced around quickly. There were two crossed swords at the foot of the coffin. I rolled myself over to one, and pushed it up against the edge of the coffin with my shoulder. Then I began to saw at the cords around my wrists. The sword was as sharp as it must have been two thousand years ago.

'In a moment my arms were free.
Quickly I released my ankles and pulled
away my gag. The relief! But there was
no time to waste. I could hear footsteps
running towards me.

'The Baron's men were at the doorway.
I saw in horror that they were starting to
close the door on me – they wanted to seal
me in the tomb with the dead King! A bolt
of fear sent me hurtling up the stairs like
lightning, yelling and screaming, "Ai-eee!
Help! Down here!"

'"That's Tashi calling!" I heard Lotus Blossom shouting, "Over here, everyone!"

'They came bursting through the doorway, ducking around the Baron's men, who suddenly remembered their wives wanted them somewhere else. The Baron was close behind them but when he heard Big Uncle and Director Han hurrying down after him, he called out, "So this is where you have been, Tashi. We were looking everywhere for you."

'I gave the Baron a long hard stare.'

'I would have given him a great hard kick!' exploded Jack.

'I would have cut out his organs and put them in a canopic jar!' cried Angus Figment.

'What's a canopic jar?' asked Jack.

'The thing was,' Tashi went on, 'I had no real proof that the Baron had been stealing from the tomb and meant to kill me. There was nothing concrete, really, so when I finally answered him, I said, "Yes, this is where I've been," and raising my voice so that everyone could hear, "and before I found the King's tomb, I came across a big sack of golden goblets. You'll find it over there, buried by the last two warriors."

'The Baron's jaw dropped. "What a clever Tashi," he said quietly.

'But Director Han paid no attention
to them. He was skipping about the secret
tomb, crooning with delight over the richly
decorated burial chamber and the jade suit.'

'So it was you, Tashi, who made the
most important find,' crowed Jack. 'Just
think, the *King's* tomb.'

'Well,' said Tashi modestly, 'the inner
tomb did make the find complete. Director
Han was given a promotion and he
presented our family with jobs and free
passes to the tomb for the rest of our lives.
My two warriors still stand side by side
and every time I visit them, their eyes
seem to glow with happiness.'

There was silence in the classroom for
a moment as everyone tried to imagine the
tomb, and the treasures, and warrior love
beyond the grave.

'Did they used to mummify kings in
your country, Tashi?' asked Angus Figment.

'No,' replied Tashi. 'They buried them
in these splendid tombs.'

'Oh,' said Angus thoughtfully. 'Because
in Egypt, well, they used to mummify
all sorts of things. Even cats. Of course
when the cats were dug up in my great-
grandfather's time, most of them were
made into garden fertiliser.'

'Thank you, Angus,' said Mrs Hall, 'and now, if you can manage not to turn our stomachs any further, perhaps you would like to share with us some more of your interesting facts about the ancient people of Egypt.'

Angus did like, and his information about Egyptian medicines and the hooks used for removing brains from mummies was enjoyed by all – well, everyone except Alex Pickle, who was sick into the potplant in the corner.

## THE BOOK OF SPELLS

'What are you going to do for your
project on ancient Egypt?' Dad asked Jack
one afternoon.

'I don't know yet,' said Jack, scratching
his head. 'Angus Figment is writing a Book
of the Dead.'

'Good heavens,' said Mum, coming into
the room. 'What does his mother say about
that?'

'She thinks it's fascinating, actually,'
said Jack. 'See, the Egyptians used to write
magic spells on sheets of papyrus, and put
them inside the tombs with the mummies.
That way, people's afterlife was sure to
be happy and safe.'

'How can you be safe when you're dead?' asked Dad.

Jack sighed. 'The Egyptians believed in the *afterlife*, Dad. It's like you go on existing somewhere else.'

'Hmm,' frowned Dad. 'I don't know whether the newsagency sells papyrus.'

Mum groaned. 'So what's Tashi doing, Jack?'

Jack leaned forward on his chair. 'Well, he hasn't decided yet either, but when Angus told him about his Book, Tashi went all serious and silent.'

'Oh ho,' said Dad, drawing up his chair. 'I bet Tashi knows a thing or two about magic spells. Are you going to tell us a story by any chance?'

'I might,' said Jack. 'You see, in Tashi's village the most precious possession of all was the Book of Spells. But you might say it was a book of *life*, because it was filled with the most marvellous cures for all kinds of diseases and problems. The Book had to be guarded day and night. But one dreadful day, it disappeared.'

'Who would take it?' asked Dad. 'A bandit? A *demon*?'

'Well, it was like this. One morning
Tashi's mother gave him a pot of soup
to take up to Wise-as-an-Owl, who hadn't
been very well lately. Tashi knocked at
the door, and waited.

'"Come in, Tashi," called Wise-as-an-
Owl from behind the door. He somehow
always knew when Tashi was there.

'When Tashi stepped into the room,
he saw someone else sitting with his
old friend.

"'Ah, Tashi," Wise-as-an-Owl beamed, "see who has come from the city to visit me! My son and I have decided that it's high time he began his study of plants and medicines if he is to take up the work of the Keeper of the Book after me." The old man's eyes twinkled. "My Son with Much-to-Learn will stay with me until he finds a house where he and his family can live."

'Tashi bowed and put his pot on the table. He politely asked Much-to-Learn about his home in the city, and his children, but all the while he couldn't help looking at the Book that lay on the desk before him. It was richly bound in red leather, with ancient glowing letters on the cover. Tashi fingered the fine brass clasp and lock that could only be opened by the golden key Wise-as-an-Owl wore around his neck.

'Tashi couldn't remember a time when the Book was not part of his life. Over the years, he'd watched while his friend had consulted it for cures of illness, pestilence and heartache. Tashi knew whole passages by heart. But later, on the way home, he felt glad that, now Wise-as-an-Owl was growing frail, his son should have come to study and work with him.

'Tashi was curious to see how Much-to-Learn was getting on with his study, but the next week, when he called, a terrible sight met his eyes.

'Wise-as-an-Owl was sitting rocking backwards and forwards in his chair, tearing his thin white hair while his son tried to calm him.

'"What is it? What has happened?" cried Tashi.

'"Someone has stolen the Book," groaned Wise-as-an-Owl. "We have

searched the house a dozen times. It's just
disappeared. Yesterday we were studying
the cure for warts and wax-in-the-ear
when there was a shuffling noise outside.
We went to investigate and when we came
back, the Book – which I had left right
here on the desk – was gone!"

'He slumped down on his stool. "I have
spent a lifetime studying it, Tashi, but
there are always new cures to find in the

Book, new spells to help poor souls –
whatever will we do?"

'Tashi came close and put his hand
on the old man's shoulder. "I will find
the Book for you, Wise-as-an-Owl,"
he promised.

'As Tashi was walking home, he was
so deep in thought he didn't hear Lotus
Blossom and Ah Chu running up behind
him until they were almost on top of him.
He shoved them off, saying gruffly, "I can't
come and play now!"

'Lotus Blossom shoved him back so hard that Tashi stumbled. "Why so high and mighty, Lord Tashi?"

'"Leave him alone," said Ah Chu. "You can see there's something wrong with Tashi if you'd just bother to look. He probably hasn't had his lunch yet and his stomach is growling. Mine is."

'Tashi couldn't help smiling then, and he quickly told them the trouble.

'"Oh that's the worst thing I ever heard!" cried Lotus Blossom. "We'll help you."

'"Good," said Tashi. He was relieved. "We can split up and ask all through the

village if anyone has seen a stranger
wandering about. Meet me back at my
place after lunch."

'As Lotus Blossom turned to go, she
whispered, "Sorry."

'"You can't help having sharp elbows,"
said Tashi.

'Lotus Blossom grinned and ran off.

'Neither Tashi nor Ah Chu could find
word of anyone strange about the village,
but Lotus Blossom did learn something.
She had been out to see Granny White
Eyes, who always knew what was going
on in the village. And sure enough, Granny
told Lotus Blossom the bad news.

'"Tashi's Uncle Tiki Pu is back. The cobbler, Not Yet, saw him on the road passing Wise-as-an-Owl's house."

'"Oh, no!" moaned Tashi. "That Tiki Pu would sell his own grandmother for a jar of honey."

'But Lotus Blossom was looking at him steadily. "Will you be going after him, Tashi?"

'When Tashi nodded, she nudged Ah Chu. "Then we'll be coming with you. After all, the Book is precious to the whole valley."

'"Thank you," said Tashi, a bit awkwardly. "We'd better start out right away. He'll be heading back to the city I should think."

'Ah Chu cleared his throat. "Um, I'll just hurry home and get some food together. It's going to be a long afternoon and I smelt something really good being cooked this morning. Be back in ten minutes."

'Tashi couldn't carry both Lotus Blossom and Ah Chu on his magic shoes, so the three friends shared out Ah Chu's baskets and set off on foot.

'They walked quickly but it was almost dinner time before they came across Tiki Pu standing on the river bank. He was deep in conversation with one of the river pirates, and he seemed very busy winking and grinning.

'Tashi sprang forward but, to his
surprise, it was the pirate who handed Tiki
Pu a bulky parcel and pocketed a bag of
coins in return. Whatever he was up to,
Tiki Pu wasn't selling the Book of Spells.

'They waited until Tiki Pu was alone and then Tashi ran after him and told him about the missing Book.

'"Did you see anything suspicious as you passed Wise-as-an-Owl's house this morning, Uncle?"

'Tiki Pu looked thoughtful and stroked his nose. "What will you give me if I tell you?"

'"Poor Tashi," Lotus Blossom whispered loudly to Ah Chu, "having an uncle like Tiki Pu."

'Tiki Pu coughed and said loudly, "Ha ha, can't you take a joke, Tashi? Where's the fun if we can't have a joke amongst friends? Yes, well, the only person I saw on the road was . . . the Baron."

'"Thank you, Uncle." Tashi swung round to his friends. "Let's go. I should have guessed. If something precious is missing, who needs suspicious strangers when we have our very own Baron at home?"

'"You thought *I'd* taken it, didn't you?" Tiki Pu said as they turned to go.

'Tashi smiled guiltily as he waved goodbye, but Tiki Pu just shrugged.

'"He's probably annoyed he didn't think of stealing it himself," Lotus Blossom sniffed.

'They were lucky enough to get a lift back to the village with a passing boat, sharing Ah Chu's delicious sticky-rice cakes and lychees with the boatman.

'"It will be quite dark before we get back to the Baron's house," Lotus Blossom said presently. They thought about this for a moment.

'Tashi nodded. "Yes, and I just hope there won't be any white tigers in his cellar this time."

'Ah Chu choked on his rice cake.

'They crept cautiously through the Baron's gardens, flinching at shadows. Ah Chu held Lotus Blossom's hand – so that she wouldn't be frightened.

'They reached the Baron's window and peered in.

'There he was, sitting at his great carved table. And what do you think he had before him? The red leather Book of Spells. The brass clasp had been broken with a poker, which lay on the table beside him, and now the Baron took a deep breath and opened the Book.

'The three friends watched his face. His jaw dropped. He turned the page. A vein began to swell on his forehead. The Baron's thick finger flipped page after page and his rage mounted, until at last he flung the Book on the floor and jumped on it. Tashi slid over the windowsill and stepped into the room.

'"Good evening, Baron. You look upset."

'"The pages are all blank!" spluttered the Baron. "There isn't a single word in the whole Book."

'"No," said Tashi. "That's because you didn't open it with the golden key that Wise-as-an-Owl wears around his neck. If the Book is opened without it, the words fade right off the pages."

'The Baron gaped at Tashi and sank down heavily onto his chair.

'"How could you?" Tashi burst out angrily. "How could you steal such a precious thing that is used to help all the village?"

'"Why shouldn't I?" shouted the Baron. "Why should Wise-as-an-Owl have it, just because his father had it before him? He never made a penny out of it; he doesn't deserve it."

'Tashi looked at him in wonder. It was no use talking to such a man. He picked up the Book but the Baron grabbed it out of his hands.

'"If I can't use it," shouted the Baron, "nobody will. It can burn!" And he ran to the fire.

'Tashi jumped after him, grabbing his arms, trying to reach the Book, but the Baron held it above his head.

'"You'd better let me take it back quickly, Baron," said Tashi, trying to stop the quiver in his voice. "My friends have gone up to the village to tell everyone that the Book has been found."

'Lotus Blossom and Ah Chu, who'd been peeping over the windowsill, quickly ducked their heads down.

'"We don't want a lot of people hearing that you had *stolen* it," Tashi said softly.

'The Baron lowered his arms. He thought about that. "What about the clasp? It's broken."

'"I'll take it to Not Yet. He mends locks as well as shoes these days and, if you pay him well, he might break the habit of a lifetime and do it straightaway."

'In no time at all, the Baron had agreed, Not Yet had set to work, and the Book was back in Wise-as-an-Owl's trembling hands.

'Tashi and his friends watched anxiously as he slipped his key into the brass lock and turned it. The Book fell open. White, blank pages . . . at first. Then slowly, as they watched, faint markings appeared; a moment more and clear black letters marched boldly up and down the pages.

'The knowledge was back where it belonged.'

'Ah,' sighed Mum with satisfaction.

'What beats me though,' said Dad, pounding his knee, 'is how that crook of a Baron stays out of jail!'

Jack smiled. 'Don't worry, Dad. I'm sure there'll be justice in the *afterlife*.'

Dad snorted and went to find a pillow to punch.

# Tashi

## LOST in the CITY

written by
**Anna Fienberg**
and
**Barbara Fienberg**

illustrated by
**Kim Gamble**

ALLEN&UNWIN

'This lift is stuck,' said Jack. He pushed the ground floor button again. Nothing happened. Sweat prickled his forehead.

Tashi put his hand on Jack's shoulder. 'Don't worry, we're in a big mall. Someone will find us soon. All we have to do is sit and wait.'

Jack could hear his heart thumping.
'I don't like being shut in small places.
Especially when no one knows where we
are,' he added quietly.

Tashi sat on the floor and pulled Jack
after him.

'And I'm *busting*,' whispered Jack.

'Take five deep breaths,' said Tashi, 'and
think about something else.'

Jack looked at the great steel doors.
'I wish I'd gone to the toilet *before* we
went to see the skateboards. If only
we had a piece of ghost cake we could
pass right through those doors,
easy peasy –'

'You know,' said Tashi, stretching out
his legs, 'this reminds me of a time I was
trapped in a dark cellar by a man with a
glass eye and a dagger in his belt.'

Jack sat up straight. 'Did the eye look
real?'

'No,' Tashi shook his head. 'It was more like a marble, with a black pupil painted on like a bullseye. But it was the other eye that scared me. Cold and mean and deadly, like a shark's.'

'Gosh,' said Jack. 'How did you escape?'

'Well, it was like this,' Tashi began. 'It was the year our village had a really good harvest. To celebrate, Grandma decided to take me to the city with her to help buy the family's New Year presents. Little Aunt said we could borrow her cart and horse, Plodalong.'

'Was the city a long way from your
village?'

'Oh yes,' nodded Tashi. 'We had to set
out at first light. By late morning we were
in the teeming cobbled streets of the city.
Oh Jack, I'd never seen anything so

wonderful. My head swivelled from side
to side. I didn't know where to look first.
There were stalls of candied apples and
roasted ears of corn and silvery fish in
tanks.'

'I hardly had time to glimpse the curio shops and the bookstalls before we had to duck our heads under silk banners announcing family weddings and births. And the *noise* – everything was so much louder than in my village.'

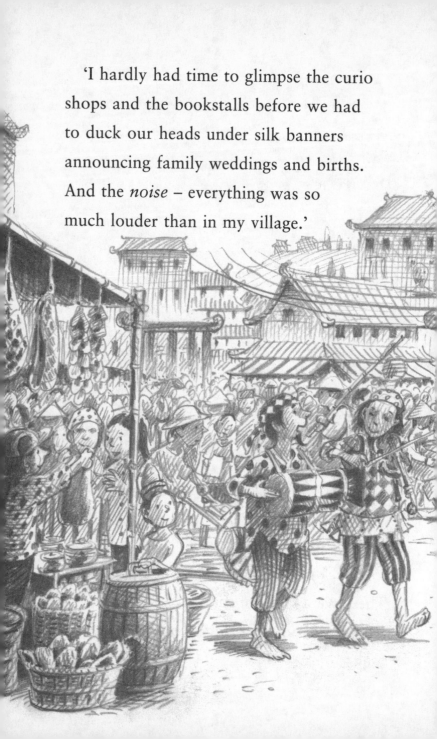

'Street hawkers were calling out their medicines, and stallholders beckoned us to see their toys. And all the time the air thrummed with violins and the drums of street musicians.'

'Is this where you met the man with the glass eye?'

'Not yet,' said Tashi. 'First we had to leave the horse and cart with an old friend of Grandfather's, and then we dived into the crowd.

'"We'll have to be careful, Tashi," said Grandma, "or our money will drip from our hands like water."

'But the very next minute, she couldn't resist a singing cricket in a bamboo cage and then she saw a beautiful music box – just the thing for my mother. Grandma wanted a second box for Third Aunt, but the stallholder said this was the last one. He could get another by four o'clock that afternoon if she wanted it. So we arranged to come back then and I walked on, not realising that Grandma had stopped at another stall to taste some delicious chicken feet.

'I was looking at the hills above the city – the sun was striking the white walls of the palace at the top – and the light was almost blinding. I turned to ask Grandma if this was the famous Palace of Expanding Joyfulness, or was it the Pavilion of Perfect Harmony? But she was no longer beside me.

'"Grandma!" I called. "GRANDMA!"

'Acrobats moved on to the road, and strangers rushed past, pushing and shouting. But there was no Grandma. I hurried back to the place I'd last seen her. Still no sign of her. I raced up and down the street looking in doorways and behind stalls. I couldn't breathe properly. How quickly everything changed from excitement one minute to being lost and alone the next.'

'Yes!' murmured Jack. 'I know what you mean.'

'Well, as I made my way through the press of people, I heard a commotion and cries of "Mad dog! Mad dog!" Suddenly, as the crowd parted, I saw a big brown dog, foam frothing from its mouth. People were running in all directions like beads scattered on a path, but the dog was chasing a little girl, attracted by her piercing screams. Quick! What to do?

'Through the open gate of a courtyard nearby I spied a sheet hanging on a rail. I ran in and whipped it off.

'The dog was nearly upon the girl,
but it stopped when I drew near with
my arms wide open, hidden by the sheet.
I flung the sheet over the dog, bundled it
up and popped a clothes basket over it.

'The girl's mother was thanking me when the stalls around us began to shake. The road shuddered beneath our feet like something alive. The house with the clothesline collapsed, and the one next to it. People were screaming again. And then, as quickly as it had started, the trembling stopped. The world was still, as if holding its breath. There was complete silence – until we were all startled by cries coming from the collapsed houses. People were buried alive in there! Some folk rushed over and pulled beams and bricks away. Just when everyone thought it was safe, I heard a faint cry from the back of the second house. I lifted a broken screen and saw the head of a man poking out from a mound of rubble. A large rat was investigating his nose.

'A wall beside him looked as if it might fall, but I threw a brick at the rat and called for help. As I worked at the wood and bricks, I looked into the man's baleful eyes –'

'Aha!' cried Jack. 'Bullseye!'

'Yes. One eye was darting angrily all around but the other was fixed straight ahead. A shiver ran through me. Not a word passed between us but I thought, "This is a bad man."

'A few people heard my cries and
came to help. When the man was able
to scramble out of the rubble, he dusted
himself off and said curtly, "I suppose
you want a reward."

'I stiffened. "I don't need one."

'"Just as well," the man snapped, and
without another word, he strode off
through the crowds.

'My legs were trembling. "Wah!" I thought, "I've had enough of this city. If only I could find Grandma and go home."

'Just then a kindly looking stranger stopped beside me and I asked if he had noticed a little old lady carrying a bamboo cage. The gentleman clapped his hands. "Yes, I have. She just went around the corner here." And he led me into an alley.

'The alley was empty and dark. A smell of old garbage and sour wine seeped from the shadows between the buildings. "Tch," said the man, "she must have gone into Beggars Lane. We'll soon find her."

'He took me by the arm and pulled me along to a dilapidated house. *Lucky Chance Hotel* was painted over the door in peeling letters. I was really feeling uneasy about this man and was trying to think of a polite way to leave when he tightened his grip on me. His long sharp fingernails dug into my wrist. He hustled me into the house and shoved me downstairs into a cellar. I scrambled back to the door, too late. The lock clicked. "Why do I ever leave home without a ghost cake?" I groaned.

'I closed my eyes for a moment to get used to the dark. When I opened them, I saw some straw matting, a broken chair and a boy cowering in the corner. "Who is that man?" I asked the tearful boy. "What does he want with us?"

"'He's going to sell us to work in the salt mines,' sniffed the boy, 'and that'll be the end of us. My father worked there once, before he escaped. He said children were lucky to last a year.'"

'I shuddered. We told each other our names, and we wandered over to the barred window. Standing on tiptoe, we could see a bit of footpath. I broke the glass with my shoe and together we called, "Help! Help!" but the alley was deserted. No one came by and our throats grew hoarse. Wang slumped to the floor and began to cry again in disappointment. I put my hands over my ears. "Be quiet now, Wang. I'm thinking."

'Wang bit his lip. "Are you thinking of a way to escape? Look around, you can see – there isn't any way."

'"There's always a way if you stay calm and think hard enough," I told him firmly.

'Wang kept up a hopeful silence for another few minutes before he confided, "I'm glad you are here, Tashi. It's better with two, isn't it?"

'I smiled and nodded but I couldn't agree. I thought it was better being alone and lost in the streets than here, waiting to work in the salt mines.

'I stood holding the window bars in the comforting warmth of the sun and noticed how it sparkled on the pieces of broken glass. Yes! Maybe that would work. I tore off a piece of peeling wallpaper and held a shard of glass over it.

'Wang looked on curiously. "What are you doing?"

'"Come and see."

'I held the glass still and let the sun concentrate on one small spot. Sure enough, after a minute, the paper began to brown and smoke. A tiny flame appeared and we blew gently as I dropped bits of matting on it. Gradually I added splinters, then pieces of broken chair until there was a good blaze going and the walls were smouldering.

'Using Wang's jacket, I fanned the smoke out through the broken window. The house remained silent. My heart began to thud. Smoke was thickening all around us. I told Wang to pull his shirt up over his nose and mouth. My eyes were streaming and every time I breathed, my throat stung. Oh, maybe I'd done the worst thing – maybe we'd finish up being smoked like pieces of pork! Then we heard shouts and the sound of running footsteps.

'"Quick!" I grabbed Wang's arm. "Come over here against the wall."

'We were just in time. The door burst open and two men ran in and began to beat the flames with their coats. They didn't see us behind the door. Wang and I slipped out while their backs were turned.

'We raced up the stairs to the open front door – to freedom. But as we were about to leap out into the blue daylight, the doorway darkened. It was blocked by an enormous man standing there with folded arms.

'As I gazed up into the man's cold hard face, I saw only one eye looking back at me.'

'The man you dug out of the rubble!' cried Jack.

Tashi nodded. 'The muscles in his arms were hard as steel. His hand reached down to his belt and pulled out a silver dagger. I forced my gaze away from the dagger and stared straight up into his fierce snapping eye. I clenched my jaw and said quietly, "Now, sir, I *do* need my reward."

'We glared at each other for a long moment. Wang was whimpering behind me. I saw the man's eye glitter. And then he stepped aside and motioned for us to pass.

'"My debt is paid," he said.

'We raced past him and out into the cool fresh air, never stopping until we were back amongst the bustling crowds.

'Wang thanked me again and again and
wanted me to come home with him, but
I heard the clock striking the hours. Four
o'clock. I looked about. Yes, there was
the clock tower, and now I remembered –
the music box stall was close by it.
I quickly told Wang that my grandmother
would be waiting for me, and ran off.

'Keeping the tall tower in sight, I wove my way through the streets, and sure enough, I found Grandma beside the stall, peering anxiously at the passing people.

'"Oh, there you are at last, Tashi! Fancy leaving me to carry these heavy parcels by myself."

'"Sorry, Grandma," I said. I took her bags and hugged her. "I was held up."'

The boys sat in the quiet of the lift and then Jack said, 'I know how Wang felt, though.'

'What do you mean?'

'Well, what he said about being together. When you're stuck in a tight spot, it seems much less scary with two of you.'

Tashi nodded and together they looked at the great steel doors.

'But I'm still busting,' Jack confided. 'Do you need to go?'

'No,' Tashi shook his head. 'My mother says I'm like a camel. I can hold on practically forever. But see, there's a trick to it – you just have to train your mind and imagine you are somewhere completely different. For instance, I was still far away, thinking of what happened after our trip to the city.'

'You and Grandma went home and
had a big delicious dinner I suppose,'
said Jack. 'And before you went to bed,'
he added, a bit desperately, 'you went
to the toilet in peace.'

'Not exactly,' said Tashi. 'See it was
like this . . .'

## ON THE WAY HOME

'Just a minute, did you hear something?'
Jack asked. 'Hold your breath.'

The two boys sat in the lift, listening.

'Nothing,' sighed Jack, cracking his
knuckles. 'We'll be trapped here forever.'

'No, it won't be long now,' said Tashi.
'I can feel it in my bones.'

'Which ones?'

'My left leg. It sort of tingles, deep in
my kneebone, when something's about
to happen.'

'Did it tingle like that on the way
home from the city?'

'Oh yes,' said Tashi, 'but not until dark fell. You see, while I was being kidnapped, Grandma had been very busy shopping. "Oh Tashi," she cried. "This city is such a treasure chest!" She was tired – there was city dust caked into her frown lines – but her eyes were gleaming with happiness.

'"We should be starting for home now, Grandma," I said, noticing how low the sun sat in the sky. "You know the road through the forest is lonely and famous for brigands."

'"Yes, yes," she agreed, "but just look at these presents, quick, before we go."

'You should have seen the things Grandma had bought. She'd found a wonderful shop with musical instruments and, with the money she had been saving just for me, she'd bought a silver flute. We kept opening and reopening our parcels, forgetting about the time, listening to the music boxes and trying out the flute, and the ivory combs in Grandma's hair.

'At last, seeing our shadows long on the ground, we loaded our shopping into the cart and climbed in after it. Grandma passed me a flaky bun and clicked her tongue at Plodalong who snorted and slowly moved off.

'The smells and sounds of the city faded, and soon there was only the noise of our wheels creaking over the dirt. We went quite a way in silence, and I watched the trees turning inky-black against the sky. Grandma flicked for Plodalong to quicken his pace, and he did, for a few steps.

'"He's not as frisky as he used to be," said Grandma, and I smiled at the thought of Plodalong ever being frisky. It seemed the effort was too much for him because he stumbled and slowed down even more.

'"We'll never get home before dark," Grandma fretted. "Perhaps we should stay the night at the inn up ahead."

'The inn didn't look very inviting. An unkempt fellow with his shirt buttoned up the wrong way opened the door, and I was even less happy to go in. The man looked like a brigand, but Grandma was already asking for two beds for the night. The brigand (I was quite right) waved us into a large room with some bare tables and a few hard chairs.

'"Make yourselves comfortable, please do," he grinned. "Some tea for our guests, Fearless," he growled to one of his companions.

'"Right away, Ferocious," the other replied.

'"Those are unusual names, sir," remarked Grandma mildly.

'"They are well-earned, madam," smirked Ferocious.

'"And you, sir, what is your name?" Grandma turned to the third man who slouched in the doorway, drinking something dark from a bottle.

'"He hasn't earned his name yet,"
growled Fearless. "We call him No
Name."

'"I see." Grandma introduced herself as
she sat down on one of the hard chairs.
But the two brigands weren't paying any
attention. They were discussing the
ransom money they were going to ask
for us, their guests!

'"Excuse me," said Grandma, "we
couldn't help overhearing. I can't believe
you would be so cruel to us. We have
never done you any harm."

'The brigands looked surprised and
shuffled their feet.

'"In any case," Grandma went on, "I'm afraid you'll not find anyone in our village with the money to pay a ransom for Tashi and me." And when we told them the name of our village, they agreed that no one there ever had two coins to rub together.

'But Ferocious had pricked up his ears at my name. He stared at me, nodding slightly, and as he stroked his hairy chin I saw mushed bits of noodle and prawn fall from his whiskers. I tried not to breathe in his smell of old swamp water. "There's one person in your village with money," he said, his eyes sharpening. "And from what I hear, he would pay a tidy sum to be rid of you, young Tashi."

'I breathed out in such a burst of annoyance that I nearly choked. The Baron! How I hated that man. He was so greedy and rich, of course his fame would

have spread amongst villains like
Ferocious: cruel, heartless men, with only
money on their minds. I closed my eyes
for a moment and thought. "Ah, so,"
I said, yawning a bit, giving myself time,
"it seems you have not also heard that
I have magic powers? It's well known that
if anyone tries to hurt me, my touch can
turn them to stone."

'The men jeered uneasily.

'"Very well," I said, "try me."

'Ferocious and Fearless began to mutter together in a huddle. Still clutching his wine bottle, No Name made his way across the room towards them. He swayed on his feet, stopping now and then to get his balance.

'As I peered into the smoky candlelight, I noticed how different he seemed from the other two – with his old silk waistcoat and his beard braided into two dusty plaits. He caught my eye and gave a nervous shiver, like an animal whose fur has been stroked the wrong way.

231

'"Come here and pay *attention*," Ferocious spat at him. There was a little more muttering and then Ferocious clapped Fearless on the back. "*I know*," he said in a loud whisper. "There's more than one way to skin a cat," and with a quick glance at me, "or a boy." He pulled Fearless aside. "We'll wait till he's asleep and then No Name can creep into his room and finish him off in the usual way."

'*The usual way?* I didn't like the sound of that. "Why me?" complained No Name, pulling frantically at his plaited beard.

'So I was ready when the door opened quietly that night. I was hiding behind a cupboard and watched grimly while No Name tip-toed (*he* didn't want to be turned to stone) into the room. He wasn't swaying on his feet now, but I saw his hands tremble as he pulled a pistol from

his belt and pointed it at the bump in the
bed clothes. "The Gods forgive me,"
he moaned as he pulled the trigger.

'BANG! Had he missed? No Name edged further into the room. No he hadn't: a red stain was seeping through the sheets. Mumbling to himself he staggered out of the room, leaving me to clean up the ripe tomatoes I had thoughtfully settled on the pillow and under the bedclothes.

'The next morning I bounced into the kitchen. "Mmn, that smells good."

'The brigands dropped their chopsticks and stared. They hurried to fill my bowl with rice porridge before they dragged No Name away into the far corner. "I did, I *did*," I heard him protesting.

'"Well, we'll have to do something quickly," Ferocious hissed. "Blackheart is coming tomorrow and he won't want to find unfinished business here." Ferocious was twisting his shirt buttons. No Name grew so pale he looked as if he might pass out.

'In the early evening when the robbers were preparing dinner, Fearless whispered to No Name, "Have you got it?" No Name nodded and slipped a paper cone into his hand. I was on my guard at once.

'Fearless poured the soup into the bowls and sure enough, I saw that some powder was tipped into mine. I jumped up and made a fuss about helping Grandma to her chair and collecting her soup, and in the confusion I swapped Ferocious's bowl with mine.

'That night I smiled to myself as I heard groans and curses ("You could have killed me!") from the brigands' room. I wasn't surprised when, just after dawn, I learned that Ferocious was feeling poorly and didn't want breakfast.

'All morning Fearless and No Name grew more and more agitated as they waited for Blackheart to arrive. There were three wine bottles lined up on the great table and they were nearly empty. No Name paced up and down, tapping the bottles with his chopsticks, making a tune.

'"If you don't stop that," Fearless
finally shouted, "I'll cut off your piddling
plaits and stuff them up your noseholes!"

'No Name sank onto a chair. He
rocked himself and stared at the floor.
When Ferocious came in, holding his
stomach, I moved closer to hear snatches
of their conversation.

'"Everything hurts," Ferocious groaned, and closed his eyes.

'"But what will Blackheart say about the boy?" whined Fearless. "You know what he does to people who ..."

'"How were *we* to know?"

'"A boy who turns people to *stone* ..."

'A feeling of dread stole over me, too. It was cold and clammy, like the hand of a ghost, and it reached inside and twisted my stomach. Blackheart, I was sure, would not be so easy to trick.

'By the time we heard a horse approaching the inn, No Name was rocking wildly, wringing his hands. Grandma got up from the chair. "If you're quick," she whispered to him, "you could just let us go. Blackheart need never know we were here."

'"That's right," I agreed. "We'll slip out. There's still time."

'"It's no use," wailed No Name. "He would find out. He always does. Here, boy," he turned to me, "hide under the table while I think."

'The door flew open.

'"Why was no one ready to take my horse?" thundered Blackheart.

'Grandma's hands flew to her face. Striding through the doorway was a giant of a man. He had the cruellest snarl of a mouth I had ever seen. This was a face that knew no pity. Blackheart didn't notice Grandma standing against the wall. He was dragging No Name outside to gather up his boxes of loot and plunder.

'While they were gone I came out from under the table. "Oh dear, now I have seen your master, I am really very sorry for you all."

'Ferocious and Fearless gaped at me. "You're sorry for *us*?"

'"Yes, he reminds me exactly of a pirate who once captured me. He was pitiless too, and when he was told that I could turn his enemies to stone at a touch, he didn't know whether to believe it or not. So do you know what he did?"

'Ferocious and Fearless looked at me uneasily. "Well, what did he do then?"

'"He made his men touch me, one by one. Slowly their limbs turned to marble, then their bodies. They cried for mercy but it was too late; their lips froze and their poor despairing eyes looked to me for help. But once touched, there was nothing I could do. You can see their marble figures to this day by the well in our village."

'Ferocious shuddered. "Quick," he said, "out you go, out the back door. Your horse and cart are down the track under the trees. We'll keep Blackheart busy until you're out of sight."

'Grandma and I slipped out and scrambled into the cart. Almost as if he knew, Plodalong set off at a smart trot, happy as we were to leave the inn behind.

'Grandma flicked the reins. "It was lucky you had that good idea, Tashi. I hope Ferocious doesn't ever come to our village looking for the marble statues."

'I laughed. "I don't think he will. In any case, I've already made up a good reason for them being gone."

'Grandma tweaked my ear. "What a clever Tashi!"

Jack grinned at his friend. '*Did* you ever see the brigands again?'

'Only No Name. But he wasn't a brigand anymore when I spotted him.'

'What was he doing?'

'Juggling firesticks on a high wire.'

Jack's mouth fell open in surprise. 'Didn't he fall off?'

Tashi shook his head. 'No, he'd given up the drink. Said he didn't need it now that he was doing what he'd always loved best.'

'What, balancing on a high wire?'

'That's right. He was once a travelling acrobat, you see, and he'd left home very young to see the world. But it wasn't long before he got lost in the city, just like I did, and he fell in with thieves and brigands.'

In the thoughtful silence, the two boys gazed at the lift doors.

'Of course, as Grandma says, *some* people never climb out of the dark pit of greed and selfishness.'

'No,' agreed Jack. 'Like that Blackheart.'

'Or Bluebeard,' Tashi said grimly.

Jack swung around to face Tashi. 'Who?'

Tashi shivered. 'When I met Bluebeard, all the other evil men I'd ever met seemed *gentle* in comparison.'

Just then the floor underneath the two boys shuddered. Their stomachs lurched as the lift began to drop like a stone.

'What's happening?' cried Jack.

The lift stopped suddenly, with a loud jarring thump. The boys clutched each other, breathing fast.

Then a voice came from the other side.

'Hullo? Anyone in there?'

'YES, *YES*, we're here!'

'Just a jiffy and we'll get you out,' called the cheerful voice. 'Only a few more minutes...'

Jack and Tashi looked at each other.

Jack squirmed. He squeezed his legs together hard. 'So, tell me, how did you meet Bluebeard?'

But Tashi sprang up and began hopping about. 'It was too terrible to talk about now. To tell you the truth, Jack, I'm really busting, too. I'll...I'll tell you on the way home.'

And at that moment the great steel doors opened and a ginger-haired man stepped through with a big smile. But the boys flew past him like streamers in the wind and headed straight for the sign...

# Tashi

## and the
## FORBIDDEN
## ROOM

written by
**Anna Fienberg**
and
**Barbara Fienberg**

illustrated by
**Kim Gamble**

**ALLEN&UNWIN**

Jack hung up his bag in the hatroom and raced into class. 'Sorry I'm late but –'

'You were kidnapped by bandits,' said Mrs Hall.

'Strangled by mummies!' called out Angus Figment.

'Held up by Uncle Joe,' sighed Jack.

Mrs Hall's eyes lit up. 'Uncle Joe? The brave traveller with many tales to tell of secret jungles and famous fishing spots around the world?'

'Yes,' said Jack. 'He's just come back from the Limpopo River in Africa.'

'Ooh!' Mrs Hall bounced on her seat with excitement. 'I've only ever *read* about Africa. How I would like to *go* there! Well, class, today we will have a chance to be explorers ourselves. We're going to choose a pen friend – someone who lives far away. You will write telling them about your life and they'll write back about theirs. Now let's look at this marvellous world of ours and think where we would most like to explore.'

Jack put up his hand. 'Can we choose our own person to write to?'

'Well, yes. And would this be someone your Uncle Joe has met?'

'No.'

Mrs Hall waited. She waggled her eyebrows wildly at Jack. But Jack said nothing more.

At morning tea, Jack sat down next to
Tashi. 'I'd like to write to someone from
your village. I bet your grandfather has
seen a lot in his time.'

'Yes, but his English is tricky.'

'I just want to ask him one question:
which one of your adventures he thinks is
the scariest.'

'Hmm,' said Tashi, unwrapping his rice
cake.

'Do you think it would be the same one
you'd pick?'

'No. The one I'd pick stays in a small dark corner of my mind. I try not to think of it, but a certain monster of a man will always haunt me.'

Jack was silent for a moment. 'Is this the man you started to tell me about in the lift? Bluebeard?'

Tashi nodded. 'He was so full of venom, he could kill a snake.'

'Gosh,' said Jack. 'What was so bad about him?'

'Well, it all began with the castle on the hill,' said Tashi. He took a deep breath. 'The castle had stood empty for many years. It had twenty-three bedrooms, upstairs and downstairs, and they were dark and dusty with cobwebs. But one day Second Aunt called to tell us that she had just met the new owner. He was a wealthy merchant, she said, tall and

handsome, with hair as blue-black as a raven's wing.'

'Bluebeard!'

Tashi shuddered. 'The colour of his beard gave him his name. After this story is told, Jack, let's not talk about him again. I am only telling you because you are my best friend.'

Jack nodded gravely.

'Well, at first we were excited about the new owner of the castle – you know, a mysterious stranger from outside the village – and we couldn't wait to see him for ourselves. We were even more excited when Lotus Blossom burst in with news.

'"Guess what!" she yelled. "You'll never guess, no you won't in a million moons – "

'Grandma told her it was rude to interrupt people's dinner, and that if she didn't watch out she'd give her a dose of witch's warts to improve her manners. But then I saw that look in Grandma's eye.

'"Well, now that you're here," she said, "you'd better tell us."

'"It's about the handsome stranger," crowed Lotus Blossom. "I know something *you* don't know!" and she danced around the table.

'Oh, Jack, that girl might be my cousin but sometimes she's more annoying than a wasp in summer!'

'I know what you mean,' nodded Jack. 'I wish I'd had a dose of witch's warts for Uncle Joe this morning.'

'Well, finally Lotus Blossom told us the news. The wealthy new owner had asked her Elder Sister Ho Hum to marry him!

Their father was very pleased, because although Ho Hum was pretty she was such a languid sleepy sort of girl he'd been worried she would never do anything with her life but sit in her comfortable chair and doze.

'Everyone was busy in the next few weeks, helping to clean up and decorate the castle. We had big parties to welcome the stranger. All the villagers said how well Ho Hum had done to find such a husband – everyone except me, that is. On the day I met Bluebeard I saw something that showed me a glimpse of his evil heart.'

'What?'

'Well, it was like this. At one of the parties I noticed Granny White Eyes asking for a cup of water.'

'Oh, I remember her,' said Jack. 'She's the old blind lady who helped you beat the demons.'

'Yes, and I saw Bluebeard fill a cup from the dog's water bowl to give to her! He had a nasty smile. I dashed over and, pretending to be clumsy, knocked it out of her hand. I gave her fresh water, but my heart was heavy.

'It was even heavier the next day when
I visited Not Yet at his shop. He was
trembling. "Oh, Tashi," he moaned, "that
monster Bluebeard was here this morning
to collect the shoes he'd left for me to
mend. Just because I said they weren't
quite ready, he threatened to – " Not Yet's
face crumpled. "Tashi, if anything happens
to me, I want you to have my hammer
with the ebony handle." Not Yet wouldn't
say any more. He just bundled me out
and locked his door and windows.

'I hurried off to tell Ho Hum what had happened. But she didn't believe me.

'"You've got it wrong, Tashi," she said. "Anyway, everyone gets angry with Not Yet when their shoes aren't ready."

'The next day Ho Hum and Lotus Blossom came to take me on a trip up to the castle. Bluebeard was away on some business in the city and he'd given the castle keys to his bride so she could make sure that the new bed had arrived.

'While Ho Hum had a little rest, Lotus Blossom and I explored the gardens, ran up and down the stairs and shouted along the corridors. We came back for Ho Hum, and looked into each of the twenty-three rooms until we arrived at the tower at the top of the castle. The door was locked.

'"We can't go into that room," said Ho Hum. "Not ever."

'"Why not?" asked Lotus Blossom. "What can be in there? Don't you want to know?" She knelt down to look through the keyhole. "I can't see anything; it's blocked. Oh please, Ho Hum, let's have one little peek inside."

'I think Ho Hum had been just waiting for someone to persuade her. She had the right key ready in her hand! When she opened the door, we all gasped. There were hundreds of wooden chests stacked with treasure, cloths of gold and peacock fans.

'"Look," cried Lotus Blossom, "over there! That's the cabinet of jade figures that was stolen from the Baron last week. Ho Hum, it seems that you are marrying a robber!"

'At that very moment I heard faint cries coming from behind some carved screens. Lotus Blossom and I pushed them aside and stood frozen with horror.

'Five young women were hanging by their wrists, tied to iron rings set in the wall behind them!

'My heart started racing and a chill like iced water spread down my back. Not Yet was right – only a monster would do

such a thing. Quickly we went to the girls
and gently tried to undo their straps.
Their faces and arms were white as
ghosts, and when the cruel leather straps
came off the girls cried in agony.

'They knelt on the floor and slowly told
us their stories. One by one they had
married Bluebeard, only to find they
displeased him in some way.

'"My mistake was to sing while I
cleaned the house," sobbed the first girl.
"Bluebeard said singing was for birds,
and birds should be in cages."

'"I served his tea too hot," said the second girl. "My father always liked the way I made tea, but Bluebeard said it burnt his mouth."

'"I talked to a neighbour –" sighed the third girl.

'"I dropped a plate –" whispered the fourth.

'"And I fed a stray cat," said the fifth wife. "Bluebeard punished us all by locking us up. Then one night, when all the village was sleeping, he brought us to this castle. I don't know how many days we have been here, but I am sure he means us to starve to death!"

'"Let's get out of here," Ho Hum said urgently. But we heard a creak on the stairs. Bluebeard's deep, harsh voice floated up to us. Quickly, Ho Hum ducked down behind the cabinet.

'"We'll come back for you," I whispered to the girls, pulling the screen back in place. Lotus Blossom grabbed my hand and we slipped in behind the curtains just as Bluebeard strode into the room.

'He was followed by two men with faces sharp as knives. "Take these boxes down to the cart – oh, that cabinet too –" he snapped. The men lifted the Baron's cabinet and Ho Hum was left staring into the furious eyes of her husband-to-be.

'His face grew dark as a storm. "I knew it!" he hissed. "You have disobeyed me in the one thing I asked of you, just like all the others. Take her away," he growled to one of the men behind him.

'Of course, wouldn't you know it, Lotus Blossom couldn't keep still on hearing that. She sprang out from behind the curtain, yelling at Bluebeard. "What do you mean, *take her away*?" she bellowed. "What are you going to do with Ho Hum? You can't lock her up forever for disobeying you!"

Bluebeard looked at Lotus Blossom
as if she was just a bug on his shoe.
He took his time, considering whether to
squash her or not. "Take them both below
to the room with the barred windows,"
he finally told the men, "then finish
loading the cart." And he marched off,
out the door.

'I waited as the men took the sisters
and the boxes, and when they were gone
I tiptoed out from behind the curtain.
There was only one thing to do and
luckily I had come prepared.

'*Wah*, you should have seen Ho Hum
jump as I stepped through the wall.

'"Where did you come from, Tashi?"
she gasped.

'"I never did trust that Bluebeard, so I
brought my magic shoes and these ghost
cakes, in case," I told her.

'We explained to Ho Hum how easy it
is to walk through walls once you've eaten
a piece of ghost cake. But then we had to
decide: which wall to go through now?

'"It's no use going through the door,"
I whispered, "there's sure to be a guard
in the hallway." I listened carefully at the
wall of the next room. "We don't want
to walk into a roomful of Bluebeard's
robbers." I took a deep breath. "I'll go
first."

'"No, we'll go together," said Lotus
Blossom. So they swallowed their ghost
cakes and we all stepped through the wall.
INTO A ROOMFUL OF ROBBERS!

'They were sitting around a table with
their feet up and for a moment they were
stuck to their seats in surprise. I seized a
sword from the nearest robber, and I ran
up the wall in my magic shoes. I skimmed
across the ceiling, swishing the sword
round and round my head. I moved so
quickly I was just a blur of red coat and
whistling sword, bouncing off the walls
and floor and ceiling like a demon,

shouting, "Out, out, OUT! Before you
lose your EARS!" The stupefied robbers
fought each other to be first out the door,
and out of the castle.

'"Well done, Tashi," said Ho Hum.
For once she looked quite lively. "That
was...very interesting."

'"We still have to get out of the castle,"
I panted, trying to get my breath. "And
Blubeard won't be so easy to frighten."

'We crept down the hall towards the stairs and we could see the open front door – so inviting! My foot was on the first step when I saw Bluebeard stride into the entry hall from the cellar. He was carrying two more iron rings. Quickly we shrank against the wall and crept back into the shadows.

'A tall vase stood outside the room with the barred windows. I silently pointed to Lotus Blossom and Ho Hum to hide behind it and I squeezed in behind a suit of armour on the other side of the door.

'Bluebeard's face was set and his mouth was grim as he unlocked the door of the room. He stepped inside. We heard a sound of surprise as he looked around and found the sisters missing. Quick as a thunderclap I slammed the door shut. Ho Hum turned the key in the lock just as Bluebeard hurled himself against the door. Too late.

'We raced like the wind down to the village square and straight over to the Warning Bell. People came streaming out of their houses and shops, wanting to know what had happened. As soon as we told them about Bluebeard, they grabbed their shovels and pitchforks and carving knives and we all hurried back to the castle. The cart loaded with treasure was still outside where the robbers had left it. Lotus Blossom ran ahead, climbing the tower to free the poor wives, while I led the way to the room where Bluebeard was held.

'He put up a tremendous fight when
we burst in on him. I'll never forget the
look on his face. He bared his teeth like
a wild dog, and he leapt on the nearest
man, cursing and hurling punches. "Get
out of my way, you miserable wretches,"
he snarled. "My men will be here any
moment to tear you apart!"

'He thrashed his way through the villagers like an army until four men linked arms and surrounded him. It took another four to overpower him and three more to tie him up in his own chains.

'As he was led away, Lotus Blossom took Ho Hum's hand. "It's a terrible thing, Ho Hum. Are you very upset?"

'Ho Hum shivered, looking over at me. "Just as well you came with us today, Tashi. I wouldn't have wanted to be wife number six." She smiled sleepily at Lotus Blossom. "It wouldn't have been . . . very restful."'

Jack snorted. 'That was one mean man,' he said. 'But then, the ghosts you met were monsters too. And that white tiger – he'd have swallowed you whole.'

Tashi stood up and threw his rubbish in the bin.

'If you could choose,' went on Jack, 'would you rather be tied to a tree and eaten slowly by soldier ants or attacked by a lion?'

'Lion,' said Tashi.

'Would you rather die of cold or hot?'

'Cold,' said Tashi after a moment. 'Because you just fall asleep. Fifth Cousin almost went that way. They found him all curled up in the snow with a smile on his face. When they thawed him out he said it was just like dreaming.'

As they wandered back to the classroom, Jack and Tashi discussed what they would do if they ever met anybody as monsterish as Bluebeard again.

'We could make a book of handy hints,' said Jack. 'Call it *A Survival Guide to Monsters*.'

'Would there be a man as evil as Bluebeard in it?' said Tashi.

'You bet!' said Jack. 'But we just won't mention his name.'

## THE THREE TASKS

'Hi Jack,' called Mum from the laundry, 'how was your day?'

'Good,' Jack called back, flicking off his shoes and opening the fridge.

'Did you show Tashi the letter you got from his grandfather?'

'Yesh,' said Jack.

'Jack? Are you eating that pie for tonight's dinner?' Mum marched into the kitchen and dumped the washing on the table.

'You know the three tasks that Grandfather wrote about in his letter?' began Jack.

'Yes,' nodded Mum. 'He said to ask Tashi about them. So did you hear the whole story? And why did Grandfather ask if you had a dog?'

'Well, Tashi said that after his family, Grandfather's favourite creature in all the world was this dog called Pongo. And Grandfather's favourite Tashi adventure was about Pongo.'

'What, did the dog have to perform the three tasks?' said Mum.

'No,' sighed Jack. 'Do you want to hear the story? I've written most of it down in my *Survival Guide*.'

'So tell me,' said Mum, as she sorted the socks into pairs.

'Well, it was like this,' said Jack. 'One day Tashi was poking about behind Granny White Eyes' house, weeding her garden, when he came across a clump of mandrake plants. Wise-as-an-Owl will be pleased, he thought, and he set out to tell him.'

'What's so good about mandrake plants?' asked Mum.

'Be patient and you'll hear,' said Jack.
'As I was saying, Tashi set off and as he
was going through the square he met
Lotus Blossom and Ah Chu. "We'll come
with you!" they both said, and Tashi
agreed. It was a good excuse, of course,
to peek inside the wise man's house and
have a look at all those strange plants
and bubbling beakers.

'But when they arrived it was his son
Much-to-Learn who opened the door.

'"You didn't try to pick them I hope?"
Much-to-Learn asked anxiously as Tashi
told him about the mandrake plants.

'"Of course I didn't," said Tashi. "I
knew it would be much too dangerous for
anyone but Wise-as-an-Owl to pull them
up, although I expect you will be able to
do it soon, Much-to-Learn," he added
politely.

'Wise-as-an-Owl came in then and offered them all tea. Tashi said it had an odd taste – spicy, with a kick to it that tingled at the back of your throat after you swallowed. But it was nice and left you feeling calm. Anyway, just as they were leaving, Wise-as-an-Owl drew Tashi aside. He thanked him for coming, and he gave Tashi a little present wrapped in brown paper. Tashi tucked it in his hair, where he often carried precious things.

'As they left, the children could hear Much-to-Learn listing all the magical and important parts of wild mandrake root.

'It was a fine day, so they dawdled along, enjoying the sunshine. The way home took them past the Baron's house and they could smell the delicious scent of flowers on the breeze. The Baron had a beautiful garden – it was a pity no one was allowed to walk in it.

'Tashi said, "Why don't we stop for a moment. The Baron isn't here and we could see that new peacock he has been bragging about."

'"Yes," agreed Lotus Blossom. "I heard him in the village yesterday. He says it's the most magnificent bird in the world, and he's bought a peahen as well. He was boasting that soon he'd be making another fortune breeding the most splendid birds in the country."

'They wandered around the garden, sniffing the orange and lemon blossoms, but there was no sign of the peacock. A joyful bark made them jump and they swung around to see Pongo bounding towards them. Tashi was just bending to throw a stick for him when the Baron came walking up the path.

'"Where is my peacock?" the Baron shouted.

'Pongo barked and as all eyes turned to him they saw that his jowls and teeth were covered in blood. Nearby, lying on the lawn, were two crumpled feathers.

'The Baron roared again with rage and whipped the dog savagely. Then he dragged the whimpering Pongo to the cellar and shut him in. Tashi couldn't help following a few paces behind and he heard the Baron shouting, "You've made a meal of my peacock, Pongo, now let's see how many meals you miss before you *die*!" And he slammed the big iron door with such force that Tashi's ears were ringing.

'Well, you can imagine how Tashi felt going home that night. He couldn't stop thinking about poor Pongo. Tashi's mother wanted to know why he wasn't eating his dinner but when he told her about Pongo, she said no, they couldn't bring him home.

'"Pongo is the Baron's dog, Tashi," she said. "If you take him it would be stealing."

'The next morning Tashi and his friends sneaked down into the cellar to bathe Pongo's cuts and give him some food and water. Tashi had found some left-over chicken necks and egg noodles.

'Ah Chu was sighing – he found it very difficult to watch anyone else eating when he was not. Even a dog. Even if it was a bowl of cold scraps. "Goodness, listen to that," he said thankfully as they heard the clock strike twelve. "It's lunchtime already."

'Tashi grinned. "That's all right. You two go. I'll just stay a few minutes more to give Pongo a bit of friendly company."

'After checking to see if the coast was clear, Ah Chu and Lotus Blossom slipped away home.

'Tashi scratched behind the dog's ears and patted his soft tummy. Pongo made low moaning sounds in his throat and licked Tashi's knees.

'Only a moment later, the door banged open. The Baron glared down at Tashi. "Interfering again, I see, Tashi. Don't you know that once a dog has tasted a live bird you can never trust him again?"

'"Oh Baron, what can I say to make you change your mind?"

'A crafty look came into the Baron's eyes. "Well now, let me think. You are supposed to be so clever, Tashi. If you really want to help this cur we'll see what you can do. I will set you three simple tasks. If you can carry them out, the dog is yours. What do you say to that?"

'"And if I *can't* do the tasks?" asked Tashi. "What then?"

'"Then *you* will have to kill Pongo yourself."

'Tashi shuddered, but he nodded. What else could he do?

'The Baron paced about the empty cellar. "Let's see now," he chuckled. "Yes, that's it! Task number one: When I return to this room after lunch, I will expect to *hear* you but not see you." He paced some more. He sniggered again as he warmed to his work. "Task number two: I will find Pongo no longer bleeding all over my floor and those ugly cuts will be healed. Task number three – " The Baron's face grew red with rage again. "And THREE: My peacock will be back in my garden ALIVE!"

'The door clanged behind him.

'Tashi sank down on the floor beside Pongo. He gently put the dog's head in his lap and frowned as he stroked the silky ears. It was quite impossible. He sat for an hour staring in front of him, seeing nothing, and then his gaze dropped to his feet. A smile crept over his face.

'"That's task number one," he whispered to Pongo. He leaned back against the wall and looked about the room. His smile grew broader.

'Tashi ran to the far wall where cobwebs hung thickly in the corner. He carefully pulled a web down and took it over to Pongo. It covered his hind quarters. One by one, Tashi brought the cobwebs from the wall to the trusting dog until he was completely covered.

'The bleeding stopped. The thick cobwebs lay like a bandage on the poor dog's back. "Now we're getting somewhere, Pongo!"

'Tashi pulled the little parcel that
Wise-as-an-Owl had given him from his
hair. As he had hoped, it was a teaspoonful
of crushed mandrake root. He popped it
into Pongo's mouth and stood back.
Before his eyes the deep cuts began to
close and heal. In another minute faint
pale scars appeared under the fur – the
only sign of those dreadful wounds. Tashi
gave a shout of joy, but then his smile
faded. He looked into Pongo's trusting
brown eyes and his heart shivered. "How
can I possibly bring the peacock back?"

'Tashi sat down and rested his chin on his knees. The minutes ticked by. He went over the events of yesterday afternoon again and again. He and his friends had come into the garden, the gate had been closed but the peacock was missing. Pongo had bounded over to meet them . . .

'Later, when the Baron's footsteps sounded outside the cellar, Tashi was ready . . .

'The Baron stood in the doorway. The room was empty except for Pongo cowering against the far wall. "Big brave Tashi couldn't help you after all, eh mutt? Scampered off home, has he?" sneered the Baron. He peered behind the door. He poked his stick under the bunk bed.

'"No, not at all," a voice answered.

'The Baron spun around and looked behind him. "Wha– where?"

'"See, I'm up here," Tashi called, "having a little walk across the ceiling."

'The Baron's jaw dropped as he looked up and saw Tashi but he quickly recovered and strode over to the dog. He prodded the cobwebs covering Pongo.

'"What's this? Trying to cover up the blood with – Good heavens!" The Baron had another shock as he pulled away the cobwebs to expose the completely healed body of his dog. He swung back to face Tashi. "Well then, smart boy, that just leaves the peacock. Are you going to bring him back to life as well?"

'Tashi bowed. "If you will come with me, Baron, perhaps we will solve the mystery."

'"There's no mystery here," snarled the Baron. "My greedy dog gobbled up a prize peacock and he's going to pay for it."

'But Tashi went out into the garden and began to search around the spot where he had first seen Pongo yesterday. He examined the grass, the fallen leaves and the bushes nearby. He led the Baron down a path past the pavilion to a large thorn bush. And there, caught fast in the branches of the bush, was the peacock. Beside it lay a dead serpent, its body covered in bites.

'"You see, Baron," Tashi said quietly, "Pongo must have seen the snake slither towards your peacock, which ran away, trying to escape. The snake followed for the kill but Pongo must have run up and bravely fought him to the death. He risked his life to protect your property."

'The Baron swallowed and shuffled his feet.

'"But all's well that ends well," Tashi beamed, "because now I have a wonderful loyal dog to take home to my family. Don't I?"

'The Baron nodded glumly. Even he had to admit that a bargain was a bargain.'

Mum threw a pair of socks up in the air and caught them. 'Clever Tashi – he saved that dog's life! I hate it when people are cruel to animals!'

'What dog?' cried Uncle Joe as he walked in the door with Dad. 'Have you got a new dog? Where is it?'

'No, no,' sighed Jack, 'I was just telling a story about one that nearly lost his –'

'Oh I see. That reminds me of the dog
I rescued once from the back of a truck
heading for north Queensland –'

'Were you telling a Tashi story, Jack?'
asked Dad. 'Did I miss out?'

'Yeah, but I've written it down so you can read it.'

'So Tashi brought Pongo home and all Tashi's family were thrilled, I suppose?' asked Mum. 'Particularly Grandfather?'

'That's right. He called Pongo his "Serpent-Slayer" and he saved the best bits of his dinner for him every night. Grandfather said that dog was just about the pluckiest creature on earth, right after his grandson, Tashi.'

'That's true,' agreed Uncle Joe. 'Dogs are brave but then he probably hasn't come across the courage of the well-known African mountain ape. Now when I was in the deep jungle of the Limpopo River I had the opportunity to . . .'